VieVie La Fontaine

Vie Vie La Fontaine

LINDA HEAVNER GERALD

ARPress
45 Dan Road Suite 15
Canton MA 02021

Hotline: 1(888) 821-0229
Fax: 1(508) 545-7580

Ordering Information:

Quantity sales. Special discounts are available on quantity purchases by corporations, associations, and others. For details, contact the publisher at the address above.
Printed in the United States of America.

ISBN-13:   Paperback   979-8-89676-381-9
                eBook   979-8-89676-382-6

Library of Congress Control Number: 2025916259

Table Of Contents

Introduction..i

Other Works by This Author iii

Acknowledgements...v

Prologue: Exodus..vii

Chapter One: Exile 1

Chapter Two: My New Home 10

Chapter Three: If Only I Knew 15

Chapter Four: VieVie La Fontaine..............................20

Chapter Five: Life With VieVie 26

Chapter Six: Hotel Ritz 29

Chapter Seven: Two Years?...32

Chapter Eight: Goodbye Germany...............................36

Chapter Nine: Life Slowly Slips Away 41

Chapter Ten: Preparations For War 47

Chapter Eleven: Victor La Fontaine 53

Chapter Twelve: The Vichy State 67

Chapter Thirteen: The French Fighters........................71

Chapter Fourteen: Our New Lives 78

Chapter Fifteen: Genny, The Whore............................81

Chapter Sixteen: The "Dates" Continue 86

Chapter Seventeen: My Mistake 90

Chapter Eighteen: VieVie's Date 93

Chapter Nineteen: A New Love...97

Chapter Twenty: Christmas Of 1941...99

Chapter Twenty-One: More Madness...105

Chapter Twenty-Two: Some Good News, Some Bad, 1943 110

Chapter Twenty-Three: Christmas 1943 114

Chapter Twenty-Four: Amélie's Choice 119

Chapter Twenty-Five: 1944 Liberation At Last! 122

Chapter Twenty-Six: Now So For The Collaborators 128

Chapter Twenty-Seven: A New Life Alone.......................................133

Chapter Twenty-Eight: Exiled 138

Chapter Twenty-Nine: Israel...147

INTRODUCTION

For many years, I have read voraciously about the Second World War. I do so with great trepidation because I find it both intriguing and repulsive. Perhaps, my wish is if we ingrain the horror in our minds, we will never forget those who perished.

One night in a local restaurant, I discussed my dream of writing a historical novel about the French Resistance Fighters. It could just as well have been the Polish. To my amazement, a man at the table across from my husband and me disclosed he was a French Resistance Fighter. We became instant friends. Later, he sent me information and pictures of that time in his life.

VieVie La Fontaine is dedicated to John Pugliese, an actual survivor of the horrors which Hitler's Germany inflicted on so many. This is the fictional story of a French woman named *VieVie La Fontaine*. Her story represents John's as well as hundreds of others who fought valiantly against a tyrant and a maniac.

May God bless all of those who are still alive today and must bear the scars of pain as well as family members who still mourn their losses. May we never forget you!

Other Works by This Author

Beaufort Betrayal

Rosemary Beach

Will He?

Till Heaven Then Forever

Sins Of Summer

Confessions Of An Assassin

Murdered Twice

Enchanted

I Am Red

Claire's House

The Soldier And The Author

AnnaPolis Summers

VieVie La Fontaine

Dear John

Table 36

Castles in the Snow

Castles in the Fog

Castles in the Rain

ACKNOWLEDGEMENTS

Life changes, as I can attest. The past three years have challenged me, but all is well. Because I haven't published during this period, it is sad that my books will be forgotten. *VieVie La Fontaine* is one that I can't let die. So, I refresh and present it for the second time. I hope that after reading, you will never forget. Especially in today's chaos and confusion, remember, just remember.

EXODUS

"Exiled" is a word which my people, the Jewish descendants of Abraham, know well. We have experienced expulsion from Egypt, Babylon and Rome as well as many other places during various periods throughout history. One of the most significant exiles wasn't from the *land* we inhabited but from this world! It began in March of 1933 when the German Reichstag elected the Nazi party. At that time, no party could form a majority parliamentary coalition to support a chancellor. The prominent statesman and diplomat, Franz von Papen, persuaded President Paul von Hindenburg to appoint Adolf Hitler on 30 of January in 1933. Hence, the transformation of the *Weimar Republic* into Nazi Germany quietly began. This republic eventually became a one-party dictatorship based on National Socialism. The new dictator desired to establish a "New Order" which would abolish what he saw as injustices as a result of the first world war and the victor's regulations from Britain and France. As a result of Hitler's leadership, the first six years of his "reign" created a massive economic recovery from the Great Depression. The people of Germany were ecstatic. Once again, they experienced pride in their country and believed their new leader could propel them to greatness as Hitler annexed territories which were home to millions of ethnic Germans. The support which he received was unmeasured. As former residents of Germany were united, the dictator's popularity soared.

The history of Adolf Hitler is vital to the relevance of this story of *VieVie La Fontaine*. Although her story is fiction, there are many historical facts sprinkled into this tale. Quickly, the reader becomes aware of the progression of a maniac in Europe and the hell which he inflicted on anyone resisting him. Maybe the fascination with this period is the desire to prevent such evil actions from ever occurring again, or perhaps we seemed riveted to this time because it was fearful and represented one of the most depraved periods of history. Adolf Hitler determined in his delusional mind his country was the "master race" while defiling and murdering millions of innocent men, women and children. This tale combines his story with the actions of *VieVie La Fontaine* who represents a point of view held by many in France at the time. Mark Lichter, a young Jewish man exiled from his home to escape the persecution and rage of a madman, honestly tells this story. The irony of innocence in France, before their world changes forever, is compared to the same simplicity in Germany which silently changed without anyone lifting a hand to help.

As I look back, the year 1931 became a marker for those who were wise enough to imagine the worst. One hundred thousand Jews poured into Eretz Israel while Englebert Dollfuss, Chancellor of Austria, persuaded the president to appoint him as the dictator. He may have persecuted the Nazis, but he considered all Jews communists and also treated them with disdain. Hence, there was a mass exodus to *Eretz.* Many of these displaced souls came from Germany when my race realized our world was about to change. I thank God each day my father, Hans, had the foresight to demand I leave my post as a student at Hamburg University in Berlin during this time. He could sense the winds were changing once again for us. Never would it enter my mind, insanity could ever reign down again on innocent members of the German population. As Jews, we paid taxes and worked hard for all we obtained. There were no handouts for us. Still, that old hatred which seemed to follow us, as the Jewish people, once again received stirring with a spoon of lies and accusations from a man who filled with evil and hate. A man named Adolf Hitler.

CHAPTER ONE
EXILE

On that day, long ago, when I entered my house laughing and happy from an average day of study, I knew. Something was very wrong. Mother's eyes were swollen and red. She appeared haggard and tired. Father never greeted me in the early afternoon like this. He worked each weekday right up until the dinner hour.

"Mark, please sit down. We need to talk." At once, I realized pressing news waited for me. Sadly, Papa began to tell me about the rising star in the German party. Of course, I had heard of this man but didn't think Adolf Hitler would amount to much. Politics didn't interest me. I failed to keep abreast of the latest news. Law was the subject with which I struggled. It was difficult for me to keep my marks high in this perplexing study of precedents and old facts. Already, I realized although my father and grandfather thrived in this field, it made no sense to me. Aware I had made a terrible decision ever following in my father's big shoes, I struggled with how I might explain to him.

I hate the subject which he loves. You see, I desired to paint. I loved art as my mother. She was a well-known artist in a small area of Berlin. A good day for me was painting in her bright studio for the entire day. I never thought of myself as weak or feminine even though my father may have. As the sun streamed into the paradise which she made for herself, I stood at one of her easels in the gaily painted red room and expressed my very soul. Mother loved color stroked with a heavy hand onto the canvases, which stood in abundance inside her studio. She also loved laughter. Oh, the endless hours we enjoyed together inside her hallowed, red walls. How could painting come to me effortlessly while I struggled with the expected career of law?

During the early fall of 1933 in Germany, my world was content as we struggled to return to life before World War 1. My family progressed as well as any at our recovery. Life appeared pleasant enough at last.

1

My mind raced over these facts as Father outlined his fears: hard times may once again call for us, "The people of persecution." I laughed.

"Father, don't be so dramatic. Have you seen him? Hitler is a joke. Not to be taken seriously!" My parents lowered their eyes. As they clasped hands, a jolt of shock ran up my spine.

What do they know they aren't sharing? Something is wrong. Before I could question them, Hans sadly stated, "Mark, you must leave university and Berlin immediately! Your mother and I will remain here, in the city, until things improve. Then, we will bring you back home. You must do as instructed. There is no room for discussion on this. You must trust us."

Morosely, they glanced at each other. I could tell, my parents attempted to smile but were unable. Again the question raised itself, *what do my parents know that I don't?* As I prepared to protest, the magnitude of his words became apparent. They were offering me a way of escaping a world in which I did not belong. Never would I be an excellent attorney like Father and Grandfather. Then, he spoke the words which rang in my mind as "honey to the bees."

"We are sending you to Paris. There, you will live with old family friends who reside close to the Eiffel Tower. You will love them and the great city which makes artists. We are providing you a way to start a new life. One of which we know you have dreamed. I realize you do not enjoy the study of law. We made a mistake, didn't we?" Casually, he playfully ruffled my hair. After those words, nothing else mattered. Call me selfish; I was. This very action was what I prayed for each night. A way to save face at the university while living in a city which intrigued me.

Can this be happening? It was like manna falling from Heaven. Without any action on my part, my most profound dream—no, my wildest infatuation was realized. Instantly, the sad, mundane words of my beloved father were drowned into oblivion by my thoughts of living in Paris.

Gay, exciting Paris, where freedom was grabbed with relish by those fortunate enough to claim it. Perhaps, a gorgeous girlfriend with long, blonde hair will stroll on my arm by the River Seine? A smile the size of one of Father's law books spread across my face. Nothing else mattered! My dreams were coming true! All of this nonsense which Papa sadly spoke could never happen. Once they sent me to Paris, I would never return to Berlin. Not because of that weak man whom they feared, Hitler, but because in Paris, I could obtain my desires. No, they must visit me in my swanky apartment in the city of my dreams someday soon. At that point, I had no idea of the validity of my thoughts as my mind bounded forward into my new world. I would never return to the home which I adored and the people who gave their lives to save me. The unthinkable would not occur because of my actions but those of a group of evil men who were out of control!

The rest of that day filled with sadness for my parents. Maybe, they understood our eyes would never meet again, at least not in this world. As Mother cried, I gaily packed large cases with my clothes. When Father entered my room sometime later, he became aghast at the volume of my luggage.

"No, son, we must not call attention to your departure. As Jews, we are still able to leave, but soon, this will not be the case." Again I laughed at the words of a paranoid old man. Still, I quickly packed only necessary items as Father explained he wanted me to purchase new clothes when I arrived in Paris. It was important I not "stand out" there. He told me it was vital I fit into the Parisian life. I laughed.

What an easy assignment, I thought as vivid plans began to form for my new life as a famous artist. *What great fortune all of this is for me!* Maybe my parents were delusional and paranoid, but they were establishing my deepest desire. Someday, they would witness my success as a great artist, or so I believed at that point.

At dinner that evening, few words were spoken. Mother occasionally dabbed her eyes, which remained lowered. She appeared unable to look at me. It seemed Father's stare never left my face. Was he trying to remember me? I shook my head at my silly thoughts.

Am I becoming as sensitive and fearful as they? Almost as though scheduled, as soon as the meal ended, someone knocked on our door. "Ah, he is a little early. Abi, welcome Franz while I talk with Mark a moment." Sadly, Mother walked from the room with her head down. I realized she might be considering the fact she would never see me again. Her walk was of a doomed person. I smiled at her theatrics. After all of this Hitler madness passed, I would take her to a lovely Parisian dinner when they visited me.

"Mark, you will be driven to Paris by this man, Franz Heldman. He will drive you to General La Fontaine's home. General La Fontaine is an old friend of your grandfather. You will like him and his wife, VieVie. Be careful of VieVie; she is a great beauty. This exotic creature destroyed the heart of many men who fell in love with her." His eyes told me he was one of her victims. What was happening? My entire world was changing. Now, Father was confessing that once, he loved another woman? Who were these La Fontaine people? The breath left my lungs as I tried to breathe normally.

Things are coming at me too quickly! After taking several deep breaths, I relaxed a little. All of these things were frightening to me.

I could not understand the power of his words about using caution around the beautiful VieVie La Fontaine. I later wondered had he not said those things if I may have withstood her ways, but I will never know.

My drive with Franz lasted about nine hours and fifty minutes during which we exchanged few words. My driver appeared nervous as he frequently checked the rearview mirror and made little grunting sounds. This small man had delicate features. His advancement into older age left him with receded mostly gray hair. He drove huddled over the steering wheel as though he could not see well. His actions made me uncomfortable. I had never seen him before. In fact, I would never again recognize another person in this new world which claimed to be mine. Later, I would wonder about the degree of worry and concern among the German citizens of which I had no idea. Of course, I could not know of any approaching danger, but many of my people seemed to feel the threat growing!

Our departure from Berlin occurred immediately after dinner around 8:30 pm. Arrival time, at the home of the La Fontaine's, was in the early morning about 6:30 am. The general opened the door with a startled gaze. General La Fontaine was a large man in midlife. His hair was blonde and very shiny as were his teeth. His startled look surprised me placing my nerves even more on edge. Had he hoped I might not come? If he had, there was no hesitation once he saw me.

I reluctantly offered my hand which had not been washed all evening even after several stops in the woods to relieve ourselves. I thought about telling him he may not want to shake my hand but figured a general in the French Army would not care. Still, our new relationship started in a most loaded condition.

Already, I felt like a beggar taking such hospitality from this stranger. Why would he offer to allow me to invade his home? What services would I be expected to perform for this grand family? I desperately wished I had questioned my father as to our relationship with these people. Racking my brain, I could not remember ever hearing of them. Already, my nerves caused me to perspire and tremble a little. During my life, I had never felt subservient to another. *Now, I do.*

General La Fontaine smiled as he walked away from the door. I entered uninvited and followed him with trepidation as I carried my small, brown satchel down a long, winding hall. The house was exquisite and gigantic. I felt plain and small. Never had I seen such wealth and lavishness. At last, we walked into a brightly painted yellow room. The decor appeared polished. It shined beautifully.

Did Madame La Fontaine decorate this palatial home? A dark maid worked quietly behind the counter. She nodded at me but did not smile or speak. Without inquiring, the General motioned for me to sit as he read the morning paper. He never even looked at me. I felt like a nonentity. Anne-Laure, the maid, placed a generous, piping hot cup of black coffee before me which soon was followed by a delicious looking croissant with a small container of French butter and fresh cream. My shaking hands finally resulted in the General looking at me. All I could think was I had made a terrible mistake in my dreams of being an artist in France. Was there no place or craft in which I could hope to find joy? It seemed I did not belong anywhere. Admittedly, here in this city of Paris where everyone appeared welcomed, I might discover acceptance but maybe not. I almost cried but swallowed loudly instead. This action caused the vague host to look at me as though seeing me for the first time. He put his paper aside and began to speak to me. To my surprise, the General spoke in fluent English which eradicated one of my fears. My English, surprisingly, was better than my French. At least, if anyone decided to converse with me, I could respond. My parents and I had often spoken fluently in this language which we enjoyed.

"I was excellent friends with your grandfather and deeply respect your father. Most of the other Germans are swine. You don't need to be concerned here. Think of this as your 'new university.' My wife has your quarters ready which include a large, bright studio. There is no need to be fearful or feel subservient. This place is your new home. Here, you may live your life as long as necessary. You are a man now so feel free to come and go as you please. In fact, we hope you stay here forever. You see, my wife could not have children. This fact has been a great cause of pain for her. I hate to tell you, but you are her 'new son,' at least in *her* mind. Try to accept the love she desires to lavish upon you. Such action will make her happy. Anything which pleases VieVie will also delight me. You see, she is my life. My wife will work with you to soften that heavy accent which you carry. All signs of the German man must go!"

He smiled the grandest smile which I still remember. His face was broad and pleasant with large green eyes. His skin was tanned and creased by the sun.

Returning his smile, I took a large gulp of coffee and devoured my roll. Immediately, the maid placed another of each in front of me.

Yes, if only my studio waits, painted in a bright French red as Mamas? This had always been my dream. All worry dissipated as I studied my new home after finally receiving the welcome which I craved. Quietly, my host studied me for a few seconds. Even though I was intimidated by the large man, I liked his spontaneous nature and easy smile.

The General briefly excused himself while I breathed deeply. Finally, I began to relax as my mind thought back over the past fourteen hours. From the time I walked into my home so innocently after classes until this moment, my entire world changed. I thought back over the past few hours as I remembered exactly the way I felt before I became a Parisian.

During the early fall of 1933 in Germany, my world was perfect although my family still recovered from the effects of the First World War. In Berlin, our family received great respect and was well liked even by a few Germans, although we were definitely Jewish. Success came quickly for my kind and gentle folks.

My ancestors had come to live in this place of changing political expectations back in 1671 after being allowed to resettle in a city which expelled them in 1573 due to political issues. According to history, in 1510 some Jews were accused of desecrating and stealing from a church inside a village near Berlin. The arrest of one hundred and eleven Jews subjected them to examination. Unfairly, fifty-one souls received sentences of death. Thirty-eight of these people experienced the agony of burning at the stake in the New Market Square. A Christian, at the same time, was also arrested. Later, evidence proved he was the only person guilty. Before this knowledge could be confirmed, all of the remaining Jews had been rounded up and expelled from the entire electorate of Brandenburg. Once again, the Jewish people were unfairly exiled from homes they loved.

Years later, these innocents received complete exoneration at the *Diet of Frankfurt in 1539* through the efforts of Joseph Gershom of Rosheim and Philipp Melanchthon. In 1535-1571 authorities allowed many Jews to return and resettle in the town of Brandenburg. Jews were also permitted to reside in Berlin once more in 1543 despite the opposition of some townspeople. In 1571, when the Jews again were expelled from Brandenburg, the Jews of Berlin were expelled "forever." For the next one hundred years, a few Jewish people appeared at widely scattered intervals. About 1663, the Court Jew Israel Aaron, a supplier to the army and the electoral court, quietly received permission to return. That was the time my family's presence flowered in a place which seemed to possess a love/hate relationship with the Jewish people, my people. Never could I understand why my relatives chose to return to this place which had mistreated them and where many still harbored hatred toward us.

My father, Hans Lichter, worked diligently as an attorney in the law practice which his father, Abram, had established over seventy years earlier. Hans was a giant of a man but very kind and generous as was my grandfather. Father frequently told me, his only child, intriguing stories of this great man, named Abraham, whose attributes became legendary in the world of Berlin law. Both of these were my role models. I loved them beyond words.

My mother, Abigail, had many friends in the town which my small family loved despite unfair treatment of many of our people. Mother was gorgeous with long dark hair and eyes. Her hair was always braided perfectly and pinned on the base of her head. She loved beautiful things and dressed with a lovely flair. My father doted on Abi, his spouse. He believed a wife should be loved and respected as a princess. The love which shined from their eyes captivated me. My dream became one that someday, I would experience the special bond which they seemed to possess with a lovely woman of *my* choosing.

Many evenings as a young boy, I found myself alone with Hannah, our maid, while my parents enjoyed the opera or ballet. Both of them read voraciously and enjoyed the finer things in life. Never did I realize my time, compared to most of the other Jews in Germany, was unique. The few friends whom I knew appeared to have the same circumstances as I. It would be years before I came to appreciate what my parents did to ensure my future and safety. If only I could have thanked them for the love and security with which they sheltered me, but I did not have the time.

When I became aware of their selfless actions, it was too late. The maniacal hatred of one, Adolf Hitler, needlessly ripped them from my outstretched hands. The nightmares, which consumed my world for years, were a side effect of the ignorance of a generation of bigoted, evil thugs who destroyed the dreams of so many gentle and loving people. Much worse than bad dreams waited for millions, including my parents, as this monster gained a foothold in our world.

This time in 1933 was my first year of university study. I loved my new freedom. My parents had sheltered me all of my childhood. Never did I experience bigoted or hateful treatment because they rejected such actions. Many Jewish friends at the university lulled me into believing I had a right to enjoy life like the Germans who often stared at us and made insulting, rude remarks.

"What is their problem? Um?" My friends and I dared to stare back at the Germans who faced us. Frederich laughed as he told me secrets of his German girlfriend. These bullies did not frighten or even interest us. Sure, we were aware of the hatred which seemed to surround us as a people but what specifically had we done? My family taught me always to be fair to others and to treat all with respect. How could I understand this unfair, bigoted treatment? I could not.

Hitler's rise in Germany started in 1933. At that time, few people considered him much of a threat, but the constant increase in his popularity and of the Nazis allowed him to raise the Nazi State. Slowly and meticulously, he denounced individual freedoms and created a Volk Community. These actions transcended class and religious differences. Carefully, he worked while his actions went almost unnoticed by most. The Third Reich soon became a police state as the SS guards controlled the police. Maybe, a few people in Germany took notice at this stage, but still, nothing was done to stop him.

It didn't take long for the SS to begin their intimidation and harassment of those they had targeted, mainly the Jews. *The Civil Service Law of April 1933* started eliminating the Jewish people from state positions and governmental agencies. Ever so slowly, the Nazis abolished the trade unions. In mid-July 1933, only the Nazi party remained. All others had been efficiently banned or disbarred themselves due to pressure or intimidation of these SS guards. We Jews began to despise the thugs who arrogantly acted as though they were superior to us. Most German people believed they were biologically destined for expansion Eastward while they pushed the belief they were a master race and should establish permanent rule in German women to bear as many pure "Aryan" children as possible. With this, the framework was established to eliminate the "lesser" races such as the Jews and Gypsies as well as a few others. Our nervous stares at each passing Jew penetrated the streets. It was as though we looked at each other with a question. *What can we do?*

Immediately after "elections" in March of 1933, the Nazis began their systemic release of anger and hatred against the Jewish people. Many of the Jews were molested or killed; some Jewish business destroyed. Now, this changing tide in Germany had progressed too far as all of Europe continued to live as though they would be safe. This blank process was denial which waited for many other countries as well.

Just wait France, you are not safe! No one suspected how effortlessly France would fall. *Maybe, for all time, people will question the French officials who handed a city so beautiful as Paris to a tyrant without a fight. These things still cause me distress.* Of course, I had no idea at this time of the horrors waiting for a man so young and totally alone in this new world of French customs and styles. Forever, I will think of my dear parents with love and awe for all they did to protect me while sacrificing themselves. Although my story fills with horror beyond words, so many others were annihilated. Their stories are left untold. The only crime they committed was they were born Jewish. Eventually, I found joy again and peace in my world of a new land which welcomed one such as I.

May the others never be forgotten!

CHAPTER TWO

MY NEW HOME

Four cups of coffee; two more croissants; and a full breakfast later, which was prepared by Anne-Laure, the General had returned to the table. Together, we stood laughing by the door leading into the kitchen. I felt as if I had known this man, who was larger than life, for eternity. It became clear to me, General La Fontaine was a kind and fair man. Maybe, my earlier fears were unfounded, and life *could* be as I had always dreamed. While I stood there, I quickly studied the magnificent mansion, now my home.

Can this be? I felt a tinge of nostalgia for my sad parents and the needless worry they felt over this strange, little man named Adolf Hitler. Did they think one as insignificant as he could achieve a stable position in Germany? I almost laughed at the concept. Suddenly, I remembered their faces and the fear which glared at me with large eyes of dread. Perhaps, I should have stayed and at least tried to convince them of their folly. They were old and vulnerable now. *How could I have just left them?* As my happiness grew, so did the ancient enemy, guilt.

The General freely talked as though we were old friends. Monsieur La Fontaine was easy to like. In great detail, he outlined his noble career in the *Armée de Terre* or the "land army" in France. Casually, the General removed his shirt to show me his latest scar which was a massive gash on his chest. Without bragging, he recounted many of his battles. General La Fontaine was a legend in the army of France. Although the General was in his late forties, maybe early fifties, he appeared to be in great shape. His robust size only made his booming voice more appealing. I thought of my beloved Father and his quiet nature. Father was a large man too but not as loud. The two men appeared as parallel opposites.

While my eyes took in the opulence of this exquisite mansion, I spied a piece of furniture which obviously was different from all of the others. A small cupboard stood in one of the corners of the grand yellow room. All other pieces were gigantic to fit the scale of such a large, open floor plan. This small cupboard did not belong. Although the article did not produce the same effect the showier pieces elicited, this small, green cupboard had an unusual charm. My eyes stared at it without any desire for such on my part. Later, I wondered if God was directing things for the hell which waited for me? I would wonder if *He* was speaking to me at that time as *He* caused me to notice something which would later save my life.

The little cabinet reflected the same pale green as the dishes and trim of the sunny yellow space surrounding me. The light green cabinet's expertly trimmed edges looked at me in a darker green color with fluted lines on the sides and small flower reliefs all around the top. It was very French. The doors had an open space with thin metal mesh allowing the expensive glassware prominently to show as if peeking from a "hidden" space. This small article seemed to cry, "You don't need to be grand to be beautiful. Notice me! Remember me! I have a secret!" I loved it as I identified with it. It represented *me*, at least in my mind. Without meaning to be rude, I felt mysteriously drawn to it. Lovingly, I walked to it and carefully rubbed the fluted edge.

"Yes, everyone loves it. This armoire belonged to my great grandmother. My grandparents were very wealthy. *Arrière grand-mère* possessed excellent taste. This little cabinet was discarded by my Mother when she and Father suddenly found themselves living the 'grand life' in the home where *mes* grands-parents lived and died. My two parents had inherited all of my grandparent's furniture, but this little object was not grand enough for *my* mother. Mark, this cabinet hides a secret. Remember it in the future; it may save your life. He repeated, 'there is a secret contained inside. Don't forget.'" The look from his large eyes seemed to demand my attention as though a warning.

How strange, what is he trying to tell me? I don't understand. "This sat on the street one day, many years ago, waiting for the garbage. VieVie noticed it on a Sunday visit with my family. My beloved wife did not identify with my selfish parents. She demanded we rescue this small cupboard which of course, we did. It appeared etched in history to us. Almost everyone who visits us now falls in love with it. Perhaps, it contains a magical spell? Eh?"

He hit me on the back, almost knocking me into the "charming piece of history." History fascinated me. It still does. I desperately wished I had received more education on this subject. Perhaps, I should have studied that at university. Then, maybe, I would not have been in such a hurry to leave Berlin and all I loved.

"How old is this thing?" He didn't respond. Most likely, the general didn't have a clue as to the age of this perplexing cabinet. Although the paint was broken and etched with age, the General explained his wife would not have it painted. She loved the rawness.

I stared with apparent interest at this seven-foot beauty. At that moment, the phone shrilly began to ring.

"Anne-Laure, please show our guest to his new home." Smiling, he walked briskly toward the squawking phone as he waved us away. I followed the maid with surprise as she exited the nearest door.

So, what now? Are they going to make me sleep outdoors? Outside, on this glorious early winter day, the heavens were as blue as summer. Wispy, thin white clouds moved sporadically across the sky. A gentle wind softly moved the massive trees and perfectly manicured shrubs which graced the estate. Away in the distance, the Eiffel Tower stood majestically. How fortunate was I?

What is she doing? Maybe Anne-Laure is confused? Where is she taking me? Slowly, we walked toward a small house located only feet from the primary residence.

Together, we traipsed across a lawn of thick, dark green grass mowed to perfection. As far as the eye could see, there were extensive grounds of turf. In the middle of all of this was a significant stone fountain which sprayed a mass of water. The statue was very tall. Peaceful sounds of falling spray reminded me how tired I suddenly felt from my travels. The gentle winds carried the spray from the fountain onto my face. It felt divine. I stood mesmerized by the soothing beauty surrounding me. I longed to remove my shoes and run! I desired freedom. Freedom from the fears of what was happening all around me in a world of which I had no control. Running through the soft grasses as I darted among the graceful topiaries would be thrilling to me. Like all other young people at this time, I wanted all of the fears and threats to end.

Why can't we be allowed to live normally? Why does the risk of another war wait for us so soon? This place, my new home, must be heaven on earth. How could any average person live like this?

Oh, if only times were different and I could simply live! Without a doubt, I could be happy here. Our location was smack dab in the middle of one of the greatest cities on the planet. In fact, we were only a few miles from the hub of Paris. But, of course, these were not ordinary times or people. I resided with a famous general and his beautiful wife. Anticipation at finally meeting the beautiful VieVie La Fontaine caused my heart to race with excitement and fear.

"Monsieur Mark, did you hear me?" Anne-Laure had a thick accent. One which I could not define. She was not French. Her sweet smile shook away the shackles from my obsessive thoughts of the lovely VieVie.

The small, ebony woman opened a thick, ancient, hazel-colored wooden door into a stone, cream painted cottage with a black slate roof. My spirits soared as I realized I had received my own little house.

This situation is perfect! I followed the tiny woman into this mystical space. The inside appeared much smaller than the ornate outside. We stood briefly in a nice-sized sitting area which once again was furnished entirely with proportions professionally designed. The stained linen walls housed Arabic arches over all of the burnished, old, brown wooden doors. In the middle of the room, a moderate fireplace allowed me to view the fire from the foyer as well as the pale gray damask sofas in the main salon. The back of this space housed a galley-sized kitchen. All of the appliances were the best French brands and displayed the cobalt blue which the French seemed to love. My dishes and accessories also were the darkest of blues. The glowing walls of glossy paint were mostly beautiful soft gray colors. The effect was masculine and appealing to me.

Anne-Laure moved effortlessly into the one bedroom. It was about the same size as the main room, but the walls were a *bright French red.* Such a different place than my dank German home which I previously rated as beautiful. Now, my old house seemed dark and dull except for Mama's beautiful red studio. Briefly, I experienced a tinge of guilt. I dared to think of my parents in any negative way?

I now have my own red room, what colors the French love! These people are not afraid to bare their souls with the brightest of hues. Surely, Mama and

Papa are well. I, too, am being paranoid. My heart sang loudly in my chest! All of this was more than my mind could digest. So many changes were coming to me at a rapid pace. I couldn't get a grasp of things.

Then, I almost dropped to my knees in adulation as Anne-Laure opened yet another door. Fear assailed me. I must be dreaming. All of this was too good to be true.

Will I awake back in Germany dreading class tomorrow on a subject I hate as friends around me cry with desolation about this Hitler character? Before me stretched a space of brightest *white*. It wasn't painted red as I once dreamed my own studio someday might, but my *bedroom* was that lovely deep red which the French adored. My studio glowed in the early afternoon sunlight with shining, hard, glossy walls which reflected the swirling light onto large canvases. These graced three different easels as well as numerous huge canvasses which sprawled around the floor. Palates smeared with old paint created indescribable happiness for me as I noticed them haphazardly laying around the ample space. The odor, which I loved more than any other, pulled at my olfactory senses. Oil paint was it possible? I could identify each color by the smell! It seemed most plausible on this day of new beginnings. Many different sizes of boar bristle brushes waited to dry in a bright porcelain pot of blue. Heavy, white shelves held books about art as well as additional art supplies. A small porcelain red vase sat among the shelves holding a tiny group of flowers.

Did VieVie place them here for me? This vision has been my dream for all of my life. Have I always been destined to come here? It sure felt like I had. I became acutely aware; I now faced my future. It was up to no one but me to make it great! Now, without the harshness of Father, I could proudly work in the profession where I seemed to excel. My love of art did not appear weak or feminine in this city of writers and artists. No longer did I feel unworthy or different in this land of free thinking and colorful characters. I belonged here! Maybe, I now lived with strangers, but my destiny as a great artist awaited. Never had I known such happiness which again stirred my guilt.

What are my parents doing at this moment; if only I could speak with them? Surely, I will be able to return to my German home soon. Hans and Abi will laugh with me at our fears and foolish obsession with this Hitler character.

CHAPTER THREE

IF ONLY I KNEW

My little house was small but spacious if that makes sense. How I relished the freedom to take a deep breath and not feel hurried. No class schedules pulled my mind. Only the privilege of doing what I chose. I wondered the same thought.

How many people in the world are allowed this luxury? My life soared from mildly depressive to joyous! I would merely refuse to think of the panic around me. Anne-Laure smiled broadly and patted my shoulder. She turned and silently left my presence.

The next thing I did was enter "my" studio. The late afternoon light filtered through the massive platanes outside which showily displayed their white blooms. The French loved *les platanes*. For a few moments, I caught my breath as I watched the beautiful light gracefully hide and then burst through onto glowing white walls. My entire studio resembled a vast canvas of unblemished perfection. I briefly considered painting on the wall.

Maybe, I should draw giant platanes to match those outside which face my window? I shall paint the leaves broad and extra green with a deep sheen! As I continued to loiter there, suddenly, sadness flowed through my body. It was at that point when I accepted the fact something was very wrong in my beloved Germany. It would take longer for the acceptance of the possible annihilation of my new prosperity to take seed. Life had been hectic since I left treasured Berlin. I remained unaware of the preparations being made all around me in my new land.

Now, I finally had time to consider the situation. My parents were not irrational people. No, they possessed a profound intellect. Both had received educations at excellent institutions of higher learning. I faced the fact, at that moment, something was very wrong in the country of my birth. My new home no longer glowed quite the same after such a realization. Even here in Paris, something stirred in the wind. It was a feeling of dread and suspicion. Although I experienced great joy at my new location, an uneasiness crept into my core. How could I appear giddy if my loved ones were in danger? *Were* my parents safe? What about our ancestral home and all they owned? It was a great deal. Nausea overcame me as I faced the fact.

I ran from them. How could I abandon my parents? What sort of selfish man leaves his family when they are old and fearful? I should have stayed with them and faced the doom which they projected. Did I do so because a sense of disaster demanded I get away? As a young man, of course, I wanted to live free and happy. Was I selfish? Forced to face the fact, life may no longer be as I wished caused me to lie down on the shinning wrap of silk the color of butter waiting for me on my bed. I pulled myself into a fetal position and slept on the luxurious down feathers.

As the intoxicating pleasure of release from the treacheries of life overtook me, I dreamed. Horrible images of my people: Jewish men, women and children who suffered so many times throughout history paraded in my mind's eye. Cries of pity softly tugged at my consciousness. Was that I who cried? My heart broke under the realization, my people were a persecuted lot.

If only I could help them. At one point, I felt someone gently shake me, but I refused to wake. I could not leave my hell behind. To do so would be unkind and unfair to those who suffered in my dream.

What are they trying to tell me? Later, I awakened with a start. The wetness on my face attested to the fact, I had cried. Even the silk covering of my grand bed of soft silk the color of butter felt damp.

No longer did the shining light dance on the white walls which resembled canvases. Now, impenetrable darkness covered "my" home. Slowly, I stood. Never would I be the same. Horrible images of suffering would not leave me. Loudly, I screamed as I remembered the hollow look in the eyes of my beloved parents which assailed me during my short respite. In reality, I had left them without remorse. In my dream, Abi and Hans had walked on a long road littered with corpses of the innocents. It may have been a dream, but the realness shook me.

I must return to Germany! What was I thinking when I left them without even questioning why they were sure things were about to change? What I witnessed in my dream would never escape my consciousness. Forever, I would carry the scars of my selfishness. No amount of bargaining could erase the vision. Yes, I was young, but so were the youth who walked holding the hand of a parent with the trust of a child. These sad, little creatures walked forward with only the belief nothing bad could happen as long as mama and papa walked by their side.

Why is Mommy crying? The little girl must have asked, but as a lamb for slaughter, she did not question. What good would it do? There was no way to revolt against the considerable number of guards and cruelly trained dogs which penned them. Those dogs would rip the innocents apart. Instead, in my dream, they walked to a large building.

What is there? My vision would not allow me access inside that dingy place. The thought was absurd; it all appeared ridiculous in my awakened state.

When I walked to the window, the large platanes which stood nobly outside were barely visible in the penetrating blackness. How could they be free when suffering surrounded my beloved people? Briefly, I turned on the lamp of gold which sat on the antique table by my bed, but realized, I was too tired to do anything. My longing was to complete the horrible dream.

What is in the awful structure to which those people walked so freely yet sadly? I feared the vision might indeed return. I wanted to visit that wretched place but feared to return there. With great haste, I washed my face, showered, and returned to my bed of down. Sleep gently washed over me, but my dream refused to reappear. Instead, I tossed and turned for the remaining hours of darkness as I determined tomorrow, somehow, I *would* return to Germany and save my parents from whatever it was they feared. Such a realization provided me peace enough so I could sleep. Early morning light gently awakened me.

I am where? My entire body ached. The webs of sleepiness pulled me back under the covers until I remembered the dream! My return to Germany may be difficult, but I couldn't stand myself if I did not. Pulling on the same attire as yesterday, I walked briskly to the "big house." I spied the General through the window reading his morning paper the same as the day before. Hesitantly, I knocked on the door unsure of how he may receive me.

Is it too early? Am I a bother? It is essential I buy my own groceries so I won't be a bother to the La Fontaine's. Multiple thoughts filled my troubled mind. I felt overwhelmed and lost in this new place. Then, I recalled I was determined to leave at once. Everything may be jumbled and confused in my mind, but I accepted what I must do. La Fontaine looked up and smiled broadly. The maid opened the door with a smile as well. Things were friendlier then on my arrival yesterday.

"Good to see you, old man! Come on inside! You don't need to be cautious; remember, this is *your* home. VieVie was out late last night. She did try to visit you on her return, but you were already asleep. She mentioned you appeared most upset, but of course, you would. No worries, she will find you later in the morning. My wife spends one night each month with three of her model friends. You can't believe how beautiful they all are! Now, what's for breakfast this morning?" Slowly, I sat in the same chair as the day before.

How can I explain this without sounding a little insane? "General, something has come up. I must return to Germany as soon as possible. I have funds to cover this. Can you arrange a driver? Please? I must leave at once."

"What? Are you insane? Why would you desire to return to that cesspool? Don't you understand: Hitler is mad? He could do *anything*. Your father instructed me not to allow your return under any conditions. So the answer is an emphatic 'NO!' I am sorry, old man, but I can't allow it." With no warning, I broke. Screams surprised me as I realized they came from me. My entire body fell to the floor as tears of misery assaulted my eyes. I thought dying would be a great relief. Anger, fear, betrayal, so many emotions cascaded in my mind. Finally, I couldn't cry anymore, and my throat was sore from the yelling.

The General must think of me as weak, pathetic. "I apologize for this outburst. You must think of me as very weak. Don't you see? Something is wrong if only I can return to my home and tell my parents how much I love them. You see? I must be allowed to return, if only for a short time. Please, I beg for your help." Naturally, I realized I sounded insane as I repeated my words through spits of saliva and snot.

A sound as soft as an angel spoke. To this day, I remember seeing HER at that moment and hearing the voice which I loved more than any other.

If only I could see her once again and touch her even if briefly, but that may not be. Caressing my head into her chest was the lovely

VieVie. In her arms, I felt the touch of a nurturer. This young woman was someone whom I could trust and not feel weak or foolish in her presence. I raised my eyes to see the most gorgeous face in the world. Her scent was of vanilla. Slowly, I lifted my eyes into her alabaster face. The tears stopped immediately. I held her to my chest with great care as one holds a small child. Deeply, I breathed her scent of vanilla.

This feeling must be the closest thing to Heaven on earth.

CHAPTER FOUR
VIEVIE LA FONTAINE

Slowly, I raised my tear splattered eyes to see an angel. I gasped. The General softly laughed as he sat back down. He watched our first meeting in fascination. Most likely, he was glad VieVie entered the room at the precise moment my theatrical performance auditioned. Gently, the young woman helped me into my chair. She remained dressed in a nightgown of shiny white.

How appropriate, just like an angel. Her dress had tiny straps which hung loosely on her slim shoulders. When she bent over to help me, the looseness of it allowed me to see her entire chest. Her frame was slight. Skin like alabaster glowed with a healthy shine. Hair fell around her face. The morning light from outdoors streamed onto locks the color of gold but whiter. Eyes, the shade of azure, like the bluest waters of the Caribbean, which I had never seen but had read about, blinked from the bright light. Again, I allowed myself to deeply breathe the angelic, young woman's scent of sweet vanilla without knowing what it was. To my amazement, I spoke the dumbest words imaginable under these circumstances.

"Um, what is that scent? It smells like angels." Most likely, I had angels on the brain.

"Oooo, you like my scent?" Her voice soothed with a melodic softness.

"It is Vol de Nuit. It is by Jacques Guerlain. Jacques is a friend of our family. His fragrance smells like vanilla, oui?" The face which welcomed my stares did not appear much older than my own, but there was no comparison between *that* look and any other on this earth. I honestly believed one must journey to Heaven to compete with it.

Her small arms helped me into my chair. My eyes never left her face. I knew I looked like an idiot to the General as he continued to laugh softly at my reaction. Finally, my voice reluctantly returned.

"Please forgive me, sir. I know; I appear weak and dazed. I guess I am." I spoke to the General but stared at the beauty.

"Believe me, son; you do not appear any weaker or any more dazed than any other man who first sees *that* face and body. I am used to it."

"Yes, I'm sure, but I also refer to my emotional outburst. You see, sir, I *must* return home to check on my parents. I left suddenly and without regard to their well-being." To my amazement, VieVie kneeled before me. I could see straight down her blouse. I had never been with a woman or been allowed to stare at the chest of one. VieVie did not seem to mind. Obviously, she knew at what I stared but did not attempt to cover herself. Was there something mentally wrong with this woman? I always heard how free the French women were, but her action surprised me. Hesitantly, I looked at the General as I prepared to apologize for lusting for his young wife. VieVie did not appear older than me. Later, I discovered she was much older, but had felt the blade of the best of the Paris *chirurgien plastique.*

"No need to apologize, old man. Again, I am accustomed to the gawks of the uptight Germans as they lust for the beauties of France. I am not offended. To the contrary, I am proud to be a Frenchman surrounded by the most beautiful women of the world and particularly this one. VieVie once was a famous model. If you were my age, you would remember her. Your father is well aware of her fame. VieVie was a great lover of many men." He smiled broadly.

Is he proud of her conquests? These French people appeared a little too liberal and free. Again, I gasped not knowing how to respond. My original meltdown seemed eased with this trivia, but nothing concerning VieVie was trivial.

"Mark, did your father not tell you we once were lovers? That bad boy!" She pouted for effect. Her full lips were natural, not covered in lipstick. The fullness and pinkness of them made me, yes, gasp again. I felt as a young boy facing a momentous moment. Forced to deal with sexuality, a subject which previously eluded me.

VieVie continued to speak with a faraway look of sadness. "The General and I were married at the time. I worked here, in Paris, when your father visited with his father. The two men were most handsome. Never had I been in the company of German men. They were big and strong. It was raining very hard on that night long ago. My driver was late. Later, the union between your father and me seemed meant to be. I waited for Christophe, my driver, at a private party in the Ritz Carlton. There was a band. The jazzy beat drew me to the floor. I swallowed a glass of champagne which I loved as I danced. It was my third drink. Soon, I felt the arms of a bear enfold me. His scent was outdoorsy, welcoming. Always, I had heard the Germans had a stench. He did not. We danced very slowly. I could tell he became aroused, so was I. The next thing I knew, he carried me into the elevator and up to a room. Everything became a blur as we made mad, passionate love for hours while the rain hammered the windows of our room. I wished Hans would never stop. Besides my husband, he was the best lover of my life, and I have had many."

"Uhh, should you be saying that in front of the General?" Amazingly, they both laughed for the longest time.

"Dear, sweet boy, yes! You see, we hold no inhibitions. Not at all as you will see. The French are *lovers*. We love beauty, good food, beautiful objects of all sorts. My body and my beauty are not *his* to govern. They are *mine*. Louis is a kind and confident man. He now has a mistress who is very young, much younger than I. They love each other in a way which is different from the love which my husband and I currently share. Now, I am older; I understand his needs." Right, I gasped.

What is going on? My dear mother would be shocked! "Just as Abi accepted my relationship with your father so long ago, I now accept Louie's love, the beautiful Cécile."

"Let me get this right. You are saying my mother, Abigail, was aware of an affair between you and my father? I always thought of him as a meek man and my mother was not even aware of such worldly things!" Louis and VieVie laughed once again.

"Meek? Maybe to his son but not his lovers: I was not his first, but I was his last. When our love became too serious, the General insisted I end it. My husband's demand broke my heart, still does. I loved Hans as Louis now loves Cécile, his young mistress. A different love from mine with my husband. Theirs is more passionate, heated, but as real. Anyway, he made me end my affair because Hans and I discussed running away. It meant leaving you. Your father could never have done it. I did not have children, so I don't know if I could have left but doubt if I could have actually left *him*."

Casually, she pointed over her shoulder at the famous General who had killed so many. Later, I learned in great detail about the great General, Louie La Fontaine. He was widely known for his exploits on the battlefield. Weeks later, I learned so much more about the imposing General whose soft laughter suddenly delighted me. Now, I was learning of other of his maneuvers. I hoped he was not considering killing *me*. I felt most vulnerable.

"Look, Mark, I can tell, we are shocking you. You are a very young man.

Have you ever been loved by a woman?" Without hesitation, I shook my head. I wanted to ask if she was interested in being my first but of course, did not.

"Mark, Louie and I promised your father we would *never* let you return to Germany. We know you do not understand the dangers which have been allowed to fester in your homeland, but you must trust us. You see, you might have been *my* son if I could have conceived. When I heard of your birth, jealousy flooded me that Abi had given Hans the son whom he always desired. He often talked about children, especially a son. At that time, I became aware he would never leave his wife which helped end our affair. At our last meeting, we both cried that he could no longer continue to love me. You are his. The passion which your father and I shared could have created you. Do you understand what I am saying? I realize it must sound shameful to you."

I only wish we could stop discussing my parents like this. To say I was shocked was an understatement. Without saying a word, again, I nodded. *I understand.*

"When I make a promise, I will die trying to fulfill it. Under *no* circumstances are you to return to Germany. Louis and I will be certain to inform you of any news of your beloved family and Berlin. You must promise to remove any ideas of reuniting with your family at this time. What will shortly be released on your people will be horrible! Soon, all will become clear. It is already difficult to receive accurate information from your home. My husband receives news before others and what he hears does not bode well for your people. I am sorry, Mark, but the way of war is not pretty. Such consequences are the hatred unleashed from madness."

"What do you mean 'of war?' There isn't a war is there?"

"No, not yet but Hitler will release a form of hell on the Jews of Germany and later all of Europe. He despises them." VieVie's statements were news to me. Never had I heard Hitler had a score to settle with us Jews. It was difficult for me to believe her words.

"Why does he hate the Jews so much?" Sadly, she began to speak.

"Hitler dreamed of becoming a great artist. Between the years of 1908 and 1913, he gave all to his aspiration. Hitler did not have the talent. At that time, he lived in Vienna. There, a large number of Jews lived before the first World War. In fact, out of the two million residents, nine percent were Jewish. Just the same, there was a growing sense of antisemitism. Such things influenced this maniac. Add to that equation the fact many nationalists and conservatives believed Germany had *not* lost the war on the battlefield but suffered from betrayal. Germans could never admit their failures and weaknesses. They needed to blame someone for their loss. Particularly, the Jews received blame even though more than one-hundred thousand German and Austrian Jews had served in the war and twelve thousand died in battle. He is insane. You can't rationalize madness. Again, I say, you must agree to remain safely here with us until the war ends. I owe this to your mother. The long nights she spent without her husband now haunt me. Especially, since I am older and know how it feels to be passed over by your husband." Morosely, she looked into the eyes of *her* husband.

"Dearest, please don't say these things. You understand my passion. I allowed *your* fling with Hans. Now, you understand the pain which Abi and I suffered when the two of you clinched in ecstasy on those many nights long ago. However, my love for Cécile has nothing to do with hurting you. Over and over, I have explained if this causes such pain, I will end it." VieVie nodded understanding but then shook her head.

"It can't end because of me. You must never experience the anger which I felt as you insisted I leave Hans. It could destroy us. If Abi had not carried his child, I don't know what may have happened to us. The ironic thing, Mark, is you saved us all. Now, I must save you and restore Abi's respect for me. Her respect for me is important. It is one of the most important things in my life. Do you understand what I am saying? I know all of this is a big shock and it is hard to appreciate the many feelings we have described to you."

I do understand. I heard myself accept their request. Years later, I would look back on this time with deep love for the woman who spoke with profound clarity and honesty. Never again in my life would I experience this degree of genuineness. Later, when the unspeakable occurred, I remembered *this* moment. VieVie could *not* lie, at least without good reason. Of this, I would stake my life. Eventually, I did.

I often cried when I thought with love of Hans and Abi. *What are they enduring? Why didn't they leave the country which despises them? They could join us here in France.* It eventually became apparent why they refused to leave our homeland. Years would pass before all of the facts became clear. To this day, so much of that period makes no sense to me and many others. The one thing which never changed was the love which grew in my young chest for the beautiful VieVie. That very thing, my sincere adoration for VieVie, would last for my entire life.

CHAPTER FIVE

LIFE WITH VIEVIE

Looking back, it now pains me to realize how quickly I shoved all of my emotional pain concerning my parents deep into my heart. Although I continued to miss and mourn their loss, in the presence of VieVie and the General, I behaved as though life was happy. If you looked at me, you would have thought. *Life is a big party.* Things were far from such.

Suddenly, I experienced what it was like to harbor lust for a woman. I thought of VieVie all of the time. When I was in her presence, it was difficult not to experience arousal. Eventually, I figured this was all normal occurrences for young men and stopped being afraid of my feelings. At that time, I saw many changes in my life which made any unusual reaction fearful for me. As for VieVie, she delighted she caused me such pain! Frequently, she allowed her dress to blow over her head or allowed her top to drape down over her slim shoulders. Never, did she wear underwear! My stares of panic only drew quiet laughter from her. She was a "bad girl," but I loved her so.

After breakfast, on that first day with her, she and I retired to her studio. When we entered the gigantic room on the third floor of the mansion, yes, I gasped! It was a pale blue, the color of the sky. Large shelves filled the walls. The dense white molding etched in gold held great easels with larger canvases spread around the glowing white marble floors. The smell of oil paint filled the space. It was glorious. Gigantic, old rugs covered most of the giant tiles to protect the ancient marble.

VieVie pointed to a smaller easel. "Let's see if you have any talent, Markie, boy." I profusely smiled because I knew art was my talent. Without hesitation, I picked up the most significant boar bristle brush and stroked broad layers of pink and red over the canvas. Now, she gasped.

"What are you doing? Are you a modern painter? I would not have suspected. I assumed you painted more classical than modernism."

"Step aside, dear lady, and observe. I can paint any genre in any medium. You may hold the mantle for beauty but do not underestimate my talent for the arts." Dramatically, I spread generous layers of heavy paint onto the canvas. The brush which I used was much too broad to outline forms, but I did. Quickly, I painted a lovely sunset with the sun falling in a haze of redness. VieVie could not have known what I was constructing.

After I completed the painting in record time, she stepped back and applauded my work with genuine conviction. It was at that moment; I believe the young woman thought of me as a young man on a more even footing with her. Maybe, Louie had a lover, and this hurt her, but she had now received a youthful male friend who believed he would give his life to protect her.

We became inseparable. VieVie's old girlfriends were forgotten and left behind. As the cold turned to warmer days, we swam in the pristine waters of their pool. Then, together we sunbathed. My pale skin became kissed with a glowing tan. VieVie's delicate skin also radiated a healthy glow. Laughingly, we smattered each other in sunscreen and lotion; our laughter rang through the Paris air. Several times, I noticed Louie at the window staring at us. Was he becoming a little jealous? Good, how dare he desire a mistress when he had VieVie La Fontaine!

Early mornings by the pool followed by a few hours painting became the norm for the two of us. Then, we jumped into VieVie's trendy maroon *Talbot* for a drive to the Ritz for lunch. We would not consider anywhere else. The staff dropped everything for us. Never, did we make a reservation; it was a given we would show. Together, we dined in luxury and merriness. If she ever missed the General, she did not allow me to see. A few times, Cécile and Louis even appeared to lunch together before their rendezvous. We laughed. The presence of her husband and his lover didn't concern us, although Cécile was gorgeous. She looked like a younger version of VieVie, but I never told my love this. The General stared angrily at us. Was he? I didn't care. He deserved to feel anger.

Later, we would nap on large sofas in the main salon. VieVie had hers. I had mine. We slept for hours. When the sun began to fall, the lovely woman made martinis for us. Then, we painted. It appeared we did our best work as we painted in the late afternoon sharing a cocktail or two. Hurriedly, we dressed for dinner at one of the trendy spots with friends. Our life was lazy and peaceful. There was no stress, none at all. The rest of the world was going to Hell, but we continued to soak up life as we faced it in denial. A few weeks later, we sold some of our paintings in the market downtown. Neither of us suspected our pictures would draw such a price! The General joked we could now pay for our lunches without "draining his funds." His wife replied better she than Cécile. *Oh, well, so much for the art of allure!*

The more money we made, the more we painted. By the end of the summer, we had reduced our time by the pool and even our Ritz lunches to twice each week so we could spend additional time creating our masterpieces. It wasn't we needed the money; it was we now experienced respect from the locals for a talent which we loved. VieVie gave me her funds for a savings account. This action later saved my life.

The General spent time away for extended periods. We attributed this to longer hours with his beloved Cécile. It may have bothered his wife slightly, but if so she seemed more determined to enjoy *our* time together.

Enjoy we did! We loved each other and our life together. It now appeared we were husband and wife. I can only imagine the rumors around town, but no one cared about such things back then, or so I thought.

CHAPTER SIX

HOTEL RITZ

The Ritz received glowing reviews from all who loved it, and that was a large number. VieVie and I became close friends with many American celebrities as well as others from France in the winter of 1933. Different friends frequently sat with us as we "roasted" each other and barbed our friends with what appeared cruel, cutting comments but we understood. We all drank way too much and wasted large parts of our day. VieVie and I frequently returned home drunk and unable to remember much of what had occurred. Today, I am embarrassed by such actions, but there was a fear in the air at that time. Even though nothing threatening had yet happened, one could feel the tension; a sense of foreboding as the electrical current of terror passed in the very air which surrounded us. Maybe, the younger people seemed lazy and immoral to those of an earlier generation. Perhaps, we merely filled with dread and fear. Such a short time passed since a major world war the likes the world had never seen. To us, it seemed the world had gone mad even considering such a catastrophe could occur again.

Does the world have the right to inflict such misery upon us, the young people of the world, who only desire to live our lives with joy? It did not seem so.

Such madness influenced the way we lived. Caution, we threw to the wind. We desired to have fun and experience as much happiness we could cram into our apparently numbered days in Hitler's encroaching Europe. I did realize because of my parent's bold actions, I most likely would not experience the draft as men my age all over Europe received the call to battle. Father had insisted I must not call attention to myself when I arrived in Paris. Early on, I had given all of my papers: my birth certificate and a passport to the General. Frequently, I questioned myself on what he had done with these vital documents. If they fell into the wrong hands someday, if hell descended once again, which was what we heard more frequently in the news, I would probably suffer from execution. Still, at the early time, all of this appeared preposterous to me. It was easier to stay drunk and laugh with our beautiful friends who surrounded us. I knew many of them were also Jewish. This fact gave me comfort.

I explain all of this to defend my actions which soon followed. One late summer day as the rain fell in buckets of cold, stimulating profusion, VieVie and I returned home from lunch at the Ritz in a merry, drunken state as usual. What happened next, I freely admit, should never have occurred. Although VieVie and I had fought the passion burning inside each of us, we should never have allowed it to grow. Partially, it was due to our drunken state, but I think it would have surfaced at some point so abiding was the intensity of our feelings.

When we entered the main salon, the wind was hammering the rain in hard currents onto the massive windows like that night in the Ritz so long ago for her and my father. Darkness surrounded our house even though it was only late afternoon. An outside shutter was banging against the side of the wall. The light from the yellow lamps in the gardens shined into the room presenting a haunting scene. Someone on the household staff lit the fire in the old stone fireplace. Warmness surrounded the place protecting it from the chill of outdoors. Soft jazz music played as VieVie preferred, but the sound appeared muted by the loud pouring rain on the windows. We entered laughing but soaked to the bone due to the penetrating wetness outdoors. Even with the fire, the room felt a little chilly. She turned to me in the semi-darkness. A fire burned in her eyes. I trembled at the depth of her burning stare. Without a doubt, I understood what she expected of me. It was wrong; we both knew. Still, she began to undress me slowly. Shivering from the coldness of the rain or the thrill of expectation, I wasn't sure. I also slowly undressed her. Soon, we stood before each other exposed and ripe with desire which had been stepped around for over a year. I began kissing her softly on those lips which mesmerized me.

How can anyone have such full, pink lips? Never, have I seen this before in any other woman. Softly, she moaned. Lavishing her in kisses from her head to her feet, she lay on the floor before the fire. She was so beautiful and perfect! I didn't mean to do this. It just happened. We made love slowly for the longest time. The beauty of the moment erased any guilt or shame from us for a short period. Today, I am now an old man incapable of such actions, but I have never again experienced perfection such as she. Without intentions, my mind understood how Father never recovered from this one. I knew I never would either. My first love may not be my last, but she would be my best. There were no interruptions, but any of the staff or even the General himself could have entered. We had not locked the door. After incredible sex, VieVie turned on her side away from me. Confused, I covered her with a soft cashmere throw and left for my little house. Something was wrong with the mental state of my love.

What have I just done? In the midst of such horrendous times, for now, there was increased talk of another possible war. I wondered what would become of me if the General learned of my betrayal? Yes, the General and VieVie were free souls and boasted of their conquests, but I was a different sort. They had welcomed me into their very family. In my heart, I knew the General would forever see me as a threat if he learned of our deception.

I am a threat to the future of this couple. Not just because I realized the depth of her feelings for me, but also because she had shared a deep and abiding love with my father. The consequence of unrequited love is hard to predict. Most likely, she now experienced confusion as did I. Nothing made sense in our lives. Our situation quickly appeared convoluted and dirty. Shame followed me as I ran into the rain hoping the uncontrollable volume of it could cleanse me. It did not; nothing could for the rest of my life. Things changed at that very moment for us all.

What have we done? My life is shattered! With a heavy heart, I plunged into the darkness.

CHAPTER SEVEN
TWO YEARS?

It was difficult for me to believe I had not seen my parents in two years. Time fled so quickly. The year was 1935. VieVie enthralled my mind as I tried to keep her entertained and happy. Fear for the safety of my parents continued to grow alive and well in my mind, but my heart refused to be sad. Life appeared too short for regret.

Often, I recalled Abi and her sweet ways. She had a kind manner about her with everyone. Even my brash college buddies loved my mom.

Does Hans still take her to the ballet? They enjoyed their box seats there for years. Mother loves it. Something heavy hung in the air not only in Germany, but it seemed to spread over Europe. You could smell the tide turning. We were recovering from a world war; now, it appeared the powers of our land were setting us up for more death and destruction. How could we know what waited for *my* people was almost complete annihilation?

As you may imagine, I was dealing with so much stress. I looked forward each day to the cocktail hour and the late hours of the day when escape from the growing fears sheltered us. Many others did the same.

Unless you experienced those days, you can't understand. VieVie and I continued our fun times, but there now was an urgency to our painting. When we discovered there existed a market for our work, and we made a "pretty penny" for our art, our party time reduced. Such action was a good thing because I think we both appeared headed for alcoholism and the resulting pains. Perhaps, we were aware the last thing which we needed in the deteriorating world around us were additional problems. One, Adolf Hitler, seemed to be sure profuse suffering awaited us.

The General remained friendly toward me, but things were a little strained. No more did he offer me pats on the back and friendly banter.

Even the situation between him and his wife appeared unnatural and tense. Often, I heard them arguing when I entered the room. You can't imagine the guilt which I felt. Louie La Fontaine had been nothing but fair and welcoming to me.

How dare I deceive him? Never, had I betrayed anyone. It did not feel comfortable to me. I hated it. Each evening before retiring as I thought back on the happenings of the day, I told myself.

I will speak with VieVie about our actions. Maybe, we can curb our strong desires? Then, I would see her beautiful face or exquisite body and melt. How could I possibly deserve her? If she was willing to destroy her relationship with her husband, why should I stop her? *The reason is you love her too much.*

We painted on a sunny day at the end of the year. Our tans had faded to a mere hint of the darkness which we once sported as genuine peace and happiness appeared to also wane to the same degree. Painting and drinking still seemed to occupy too much of our time. We didn't know what Louie did with his hours. He was seldom home anymore. When I did see him, his look seemed wrought with distractions. Did he know about his wife and me? *What else can be consuming his mind?*

"Darling, you know, we should probably curb our affections somewhat. Do you think?"

"What? You don't love me anymore? What did I do, Markie?" Softly, I explained she hadn't done anything wrong, but I loved her madly and wanted to be sure her security and happiness remained guarded.

"One day soon, I must return to Germany, you know. I haven't heard from my family in two years. It is hard for me to comprehend I have been away so long." The beautiful blonde ambled over to me. Passionately, she kissed me. How could I resist?

"Are you telling me you don't want any more of this?" Slowly, she began to undress. The light bounced on her skin making her glow. Golden strands of spun honey fell around her large azure eyes. My heart melted. My blood pressure soared!

"You don't want this?" Nakedly, she faced me. I burned with desire. Longing to grab her and cradle her to the floor, I hesitated. At that moment, the door was thrown open. General La Fontaine stood there with two soldiers. We all froze. The two young soldiers stared at the naked beauty. The General sauntered toward her. He covered her with a cashmere throw and hugged her gently.

How can he be so calm? "Gentlemen, you need to excuse me for a moment. Oh, by the way, this is my wife, VieVie, and our friend Mark."

Soldiers frightened me. No one ever said my name because conditions had become too dangerous to be a German anywhere in Europe. I didn't know what to do if they began to question me about my relationship with the La Fontaine's. If I merely spoke my name, I opened grounds for interrogation.

In March 1935, Hitler established a general military draft in Germany. I felt like an imposter as I imagined long lines of men my age facing the draft in my homeland. My position appeared unfair. *My situation is most unfair.*

While I continued to party and share adulterous moments with the wife of a friend, others faced war and the accompanying hell. Suddenly, many European leaders began to understand the danger of this aggressive leader named Adolf Hitler. He received warnings against future aggression. However, Britain's approach was to continue appeasement as they had from the beginning of his "reign." They would try anything to prevent another world war. The two soldiers who entered jubilantly now exited with their heads down. I thought things would end for us here.

We went too far. The General will never forgive us now. We'll be on the street. To my amazement, after their exit, General La Fontaine sadly turned toward us.

"VieVie, I thought since you have Mark as 'your son' you might stop this blatant exposing of yourself. *Chéri*, this behavior is strange."

"Mark, my lovely wife has problems. Due to the affair with your father and the fact he left her as well as the effects of the previous war plus many problems as a young girl, she now must see a psychiatrist. Sometimes, her actions appear strange, but she is a good person. You should go back to your house. VieVie needs rest. We'll see you tonight at dinner."

"Wait, General, what do you mean, she does 'strange things?' Do you mean she has behaved like this in your presence before?" VieVie entered "her" world and refused to look at me. Her beautiful, puckered lips made little whining sounds like a child.

"Well, old man, let's say you are not the first and probably won't be the last. My wife is on heavy medications which is another reason I worry about the drinking between the two of you. Your actions only exacerbate her illness. Now, go home or out somewhere. You are a good 'son,' but you need time away from VieVie or your 'mother' as she calls herself. The two of you are now entirely out of control, Mark."

With gusto, he slapped me on the back a little too hard. I could have sworn I saw anger in his eyes, but then he gently held VieVie in his arms with love. He spoke softly and soothingly as to a small child. I watched as he gently caressed her in his arms. Confusedly, I walked out the side door, so I wouldn't have to face the soldiers. I desired to *run* back to my house, but I made myself meander as though unaffected by the words of my host in case the soldiers observed my departure. The brilliant sun above appeared out of place in my world of blackness and chaos.

As I entered the peace of my little house, I stood by the large window and observed the beautiful platanes bowing gently in the mild wind. The bright sun bounced off the large green leaves. These plants began to represent freedom to me, but I no longer felt free. Due to my actions, I felt shackled to a deceptive life. My thoughts remembered all of the young men forced to go to battle as I avoided the threat of the draft in my homeland. What right did the platanes have to be so free, blowing in the wind? *What reason do I have to remain free?*

The day was unseasonably warm. The blueness of the sky was soothing. It impressed me; the words of the General were correct. Never did I venture from the house without the company of my hostess. *Am I afraid?*

What if someone asked me my last name? The dangers of being a German were alarming even here in Paris. What were things like back home for my parents? It was good I didn't know. How could I have borne the truth? Life became difficult for this German Jew even in Paris.

CHAPTER EIGHT

GOODBYE GERMANY

Things were not well in Germany as I fell more in love with VieVie and set myself up for a fall with the General in Paris. The weather turned cold in France on March of 1935. What happened in Germany was bitter. Hitler announced the *Nuremberg Laws* in 1935 stripping Jews of their civil rights as German citizens and separating them from other Germans legally, socially, and politically. Jews became defined as a "separate race" under *The Law for the Protection of German Blood and Honor.* These things were the beginning of the end for the Jews. Such small steps while "our" leader changed Germany. As the tide turned in Berlin and all over Germany, my situation with the General also appeared altered.

The Jewish people in Germany now feared going outside as I did in France. Would the Jews never find a place which welcomed and protected them? Sadly, I pondered my distressing situation. There did not appear an answer or a way to settle this. Sometimes, I dreamed of going back to Germany, so that I could see my parents. Seldom did the General return home. When he did, it was late, and I had already retired. Look what I had done to a couple once in love, to a happy home!

Europe's last chance to avoid any more aggression from this maniac, Hitler, occurred on 7 March 1936, as another year passed. *Does time whiz past so quickly in Germany for my parents?*

Without warning, the German dictator marched his troops into the demilitarized Rhineland. His blatant actions created a violation of the *Treaties of Versailles and Locarno.* Still, France refused to strike without the support of Britain. Hitler's response to such inaction was additional aggression. Another significant effect of the Nazis was Germany and Japan signed the *Anti-Comintern Pact* on 25 November 1936 against communism which may have appeared the right thing to their citizens.

This action only spurred on many who believed Hitler was their savior and he was a good man. The Germans were ecstatic.

My people, the Jews, hid in fear and shame as they waited to see what fate awaited them. At this point, surely they were aware the outcome would not be well for them. The parallel between my life as I hid in Paris and theirs as they hid to avoid abuse in Germany was painfully clear to me.

This Christmas season of 1936, I had no idea my parents were the target of thugs in Berlin. Father quickly closed down his law practice with the hope if he "went away" they would leave him alone. They did not. Relentlessly, they threw rocks into the windows of his law practice. Soon, they needlessly destroyed the beautiful office where he and his father had productively worked for so many years, and they looted old family heirlooms. What remained was desecrated. The SS guards soon confiscated his law office. Father and Mother must have been terrified and inconsolable, but I didn't know this because my life filled with music, art, great food and love for a beautiful Parisian woman. It became impossible to receive news of individual Jewish families. My dear parents were left to suffer alone in a town which openly displayed their hatred for all Jews. These facts did not become clear to me until years later as I tried to trace the years for my beloved Hans and Abi.

The German thugs believed the Jews tried to gain power at the expense of the "pure" race. My people received accusations of being in collusion with and responsible for communism, capitalism, liberalism, socialism, revolution, *anything* which they could pin on them to create anger in the German people. Innocents faced lies and accusations daily.

What can the Jews do? They were accustomed to abuse. Years of past atrocities called to their attention the understanding of what awaited. *My people appear doomed once again.* Hope had not entirely waned for them. Britain may still step in to assist them, at least such remained their hope.

Speedily, another year swept past us. Within fours years, conditions in my beloved Germany deteriorated terribly. If I had returned at this point, I could not have recognized the place where I was born. Even some of the Germans were beginning to question Hitler's actions. Italy and Spain signed the *Anti-Comintern Pact* on 6 November 1937, as the sides seemed to be forming in preparation for another world war. My people, the Jews, were beginning to feel Hitler's wrath but not entirely, not yet. Although excluded from working and not allowed to assemble, there remained a faint glint of hope for them. Maybe, the Austrian monster would "see the light" and regret his harshness?

Later, I would learn my parents lived on practically nothing at that time. They must do *nothing* to create provocation. Germans now occupied my father's law office. It is difficult for me to imagine those monsters occupying the beloved space where my grandfather and father worked so happily. Father was afraid to use his hidden money or buy many groceries. It was not wise to call attention. The SS guards roamed the streets and harassed anyone "different." Women were groped or even raped. Such things did not receive discussion; besides, they couldn't assemble anymore to complain. There were no more concerts or ballets, not for my folks. Evenings found them huddled together in fear and doubt for their futures. Most likely, they found solace in the fact their only son was safe and well in Paris. Yes, I was enjoying the time of my life, but the words of the General had produced suspicions in me toward my love.

Is VieVie insane? Her actions had always appeared strange. Even the General looked "not normal" to me on arrival, but I attributed it to my being an "uptight" German. For the first time, I questioned my good fortune of being loved by Mrs. La Fontaine. Even she admitted, at our meeting, she had entertained many lovers. Slowly, my opinion changed for the La Fontaine's, both VieVie and the General as well as myself. Over and over, I began to play the old tapes of our meeting which only produced more doubt and confusion.

Several excellent books waited for me on the shelves of my studio. Quickly, I hurried to them after being excused from the presence of the General. Tiredness ebbed over me. I needed a distraction. So, I grabbed one of the novels and went to my bedroom for a rest. Unknowingly, I had selected *A Farewell to Arms* by Hemingway. As I speedily read about Frederic Henry and Catherine Barkley, my fears for VieVie and myself grew. Undoubtedly, we spiraled toward another devastating fall. Europe appeared doomed as did my love for VieVie. Even after the General's words, I continued to love her so. If she was insane, I didn't care. *As long as Louie allows me to live with them, I will dedicate my life to her.*

It surprised me; I felt anger toward my father after the words of Louie. Father was much older than the French woman whom we both loved. How dare he act without caring how his lust may affect her? She was mentally sick as someone who faced a terrible illness. VieVie did suffer from a terrible mental defect. As I dressed for dinner, I laughed.

I am questioning my father about his cavalier actions for my mother and lover when I am behaving as despicably as he? Wasn't I also using her? Maybe, there existed a defect in our genes which caused deception as with Hitler? My problems seemed to loom over me, but what was happening to the citizens of Germany was so much worse and only increasing in severity each day.

One thing which the General demanded was punctuality. Never would I be late for any event with him, even a casual dinner. Of course, we dressed formally for our meals. VieVie always looked splendid. Her body never gained an ounce although we ate late meals and drank martinis with a passion. One refused to dine in Paris until 8 pm or later. Our meals lasted for hours. The La Fontaine's insisted on music, flowers, candles and plenty of wine. Each dinner was elegant and distinctive. As I entered the room this particular night, I was unsure of what to expect from VieVie and the General.

The couple danced slowly beside the dining table which sat in opulence. The sound, which filled the air, was soft and jazzy as VieVie preferred. Mealtime was always special. Each one was different. Long pink candles, Vie Vie's favorites, reflected light eerily on the walls this evening. Quietly, I walked toward them. They looked exceptionally elegant. VieVie and the General appeared to radiate love. The lovely Madame La Fontaine wore a dress of brightest red. As they danced, they melted into each other's arms. I could tell. They had made love. VieVie refused to look at me. Finally, the General reluctantly pulled away from her embrace. He smiled.

"Well, hello, old man. Good to see you. Don't you look dapper this evening? The staff has prepared another wonderful meal." *He appears ill at ease.*

Usually, VieVie would insist we share a martini before our meal. The General only drank wine in my presence. That little action appeared to leave her husband out of something which just we shared. Tonight, she did not even speak to me. Her refusal to look at me hurt a little. I was unsure of how to proceed. Actions like this would be one of many such bizarre incidents in our future. Eventually, I would learn to accept her avoidance of me and the next moment discover the passion of her love.

Yes, life unraveled for us all. We fell into a downward spiral of confusion, fear and passion. Conditions only worsened as time slipped slowly, quietly away. We all heard the loud ticking of time but continued to turn our heads and look away from the apparent truth. Adolf Hitler was in power. Relentlessly, he was coming for the Jews not only in Germany but Paris as well as all over Europe. It appeared I faced doom no matter where I ran! No wonder many people were committing suicide. What we experienced broke our hearts.

What have we done to Hitler to cause such hatred? I have never recovered from actions of this madman. How can one understand that sort of hatred and depravity? Do the tears ever really end with memories of tortured loved ones?

CHAPTER NINE

LIFE SLOWLY SLIPS AWAY

Another year passed for us in Paris. Not much changed. VieVie and I continued to share unlimited passion but became masters at skillfully hiding it from the General and everyone. No longer did we kiss or grope each other in public as earlier. In this year of 1938, we could not know how closely the loom of war flowed. Soon enough, our actions would appear depraved and immoral as innocents began to die. Even up to the point of 1938 September, the British Prime Minister, Chamberlain, went to Germany to try his skill at negotiations once again with a dictator who laughed behind his back. Without a word, Hitler decided to cede the Sudetenland to Germany. How could this madman receive, without a fight, practically everything which he demanded?

On the morning of 5 October 1938, there was a rap on my door. VieVie and I had continued to enjoy our secret love and glamorous life. Sure, I heard of the horrors in Germany as well as other countries but refused to accept this word as accurate.

These horrific actions can't be happening. Many of us refused to face the truth. Didn't the General promise to keep me abreast of the tide of change in my homeland? The night before, VieVie and I had partied at the Hemingway Bar in the Ritz. We both suffered from massive headaches this morning. I opened the door with a groan suspecting the maid wanted to clean my room at this ghastly hour. Instead, I grimly faced the General. He did not look happy. Anytime this occurred, I became nervous. Of course, I knew he was onto VieVie and me. Briskly, he entered the room. He pushed me as he walked past, evidently not happy.

"For goodness sake, Mark, it smells like a wine vat in here. You and my wife definitely need to curb your drunkenness. Rumor has it you are out all hours drinking with the Americans. Things are changing, old man, you need to be aware. Perceptions have never been this important in all of history! It pains me to tell you this because you are like family to me. It is beyond my scope to protect the two of you much longer especially when you behave like this!"

He waved his hand around in the air as he presented the words to me with the look of a hurt animal. He knew. I felt certain he was aware of the status of my relationship with his wife. It had to happen when we earlier had kissed, and I had fondled her in public. Friends laughed at us and encouraged us to continue our crude behavior. We had.

Our "family" was in deep trouble. The next words from the General created profound fear as he continued.

"Mark, your parents are in grave danger. Your father hasn't worked in over five years. Without knowledge of their assets, I only wonder how much longer they might survive. I haven't told you because, from the beginning of this madness, he requested I not upset you. They live on savings which have now been seized by the German government. It has happened all over Germany, not merely to them. I am sorry, indeed, to confide this news to you. I hoped, for the longest time, it may pass. Perhaps, there would be an uprising and Hitler would be expelled, at least we had hope. That never happened. Now, it is too late. The maniac has such a foothold in the government that until something major occurs, such as intervention by another world power, he will remain in control. I'm afraid we have lost the Germany you and I knew, and you loved. No one can leave there now, and it is impossible to enter. You need to lay low here in Paris and not call attention to yourself. If people begin to ask questions about you and your heritage, you are placed in great danger as well as causing serious harm to us. Your German accent has weakened over these years, but there is still a hint."

"VieVie and I had a serious row last night. She accused me of spending too much time with Cécile. In reality, I broke up with my love many months ago because of what is happening all over the world. Our age is a dangerous and fearful time for everyone, old man. I have better things to do than carouse with women and party. So do you, my son. It is time for those of us with understanding to take a stand and protect our families. We changed my assignment to active duty. *Your* assignment is to take care of this house and *my* wife while I am absent. I'm not sure when I will return. My assignment is the Western

Front. Your's to care for VieVie. Remember, she is *MY* wife. Do you understand, Mark?"

I felt shaken, so all I could do was lower my eyes and nod. It seemed impossible for me to look this man in the eyes. I had avoided doing so for months. We had walked around each other on "eggshells" so to speak. Now, we had to work together.

"Of course, sir. You must depend on me. I will guard VieVie with my very life."

"I bet you will. So be it! I leave early tomorrow. I hope you will join my wife and me for dinner this evening. It may be our final parting. Let me repeat; there is no knowledge of when I may return, if ever. Do you understand?" He stood. The door closed. I was alone to face myself in the mirror hanging by the door which produced a blurred image of a young man who had aged drastically since arrival. How many more lines and creases awaited the image facing me? I could not understand the horror which waited for VieVie and me.

The Night of the Broken Glass, in 1938, essentially began the torment of my beloved race and Germany as I once knew. Now, all hell started. That night, 9 November 1938, seems to have been as the result of the assassination of a German official in Paris by a Jewish teenager. With this event, the arrest of innocent Jews began because of the crime of "being Jewish." Horror ran rampant on these innocent souls who received segregation with increasing violence. Many continued to commit suicide as they realized what was happening and even worse, what was coming. Many couldn't face the pain again. At this time, many Jews tried to leave Germany.

My parents' history evaporated at this point. Of course, we all realized their eventual fate. The Nazis ripped everything they had owned for generations. Beloved Hans and Abi, they forced them to wear a yellow star which labeled them as "different," inferior. Such actions made them exist in fear of evil rebukes. These actions by the Nazis marked the end for the German Jews. However, on the *Night of Broken Glass* conditions escalated quickly.

Parisian life melted into an abyss. A year later, in my homeland, the next year, 1939, almost half of the German-Jewish population and even more Austrian Jews (1938-1939) somehow managed to flee Nazi persecution. These souls quickly emigrated mainly to the United States,

Palestine, elsewhere in Europe (where the Nazi conquests trapped them during the war), Latin America and Japanese-occupied Shanghai (which required no visas for entry). Those Jews who remained under Nazi rule were either unwilling to uproot themselves or unable to obtain visas, sponsors in host countries, or funds for emigration. Many of those unable to escape were old and frail. Already, they had survived one world war, but could they survive this? So many foreign countries such as the United States, Canada, Britain and France simply refused admittance to vast numbers of refugees. How could my precious Hans and Abi have been wise enough to plan *my* escape so early? Now, I questioned my decision to escape to Paris because what was beginning to occur here was not safe. Conditions more and more resembled Berlin.

Still, I shamelessly led a life of what now seems depravity. There I was, enjoying the "good life" because of the foresight and bravery of my parents. They remained to protect all they worked for over two generations from annihilation. Again, this was to protect me and my future. Of course, they could not accomplish this. What faced them was the image of evil!

Dinner hour was tense. The General's face creased with worry lines. I noticed his upper lip contained perspiration. Even VieVie, who mostly appeared uninterested in those around her, carefully observed him.

"Louie, what do you know that you are not telling us? Mark and I aren't fools, well not entirely! You must be honest because we are a family although I do admit, we are a little strange lot." Her statement elicited a chuckle from the General. With deliberation, he took her small hand. She was child-like. We both adored her as did *how many others?* My question, as to the number of her lovers, was never answered by her or Louie.

"What I know, I can't share. My love, you know the drill. My orders are clear, not that I necessarily approve, but my job is to 'do as told.'" Sadly, he looked at VieVie and then at me. It pleased me when he put his big hand on my arm and smiled at me again.

I guess I remain a part of the family. His touch had not graced me in so long. *What is happening in Germany is beyond our wildest nightmares!* I thought as I morosely, hung my head. Were those tears gently splattered on his lashes? I thought of my earlier dream and the hollow eyes walking toward an unnamed structure.

What did it contain? Will I ever find the answer? "There is a good chance the Germans may set their sites on Paris. Mark, you need to hear the facts. For too long, I have tried to protect you. It may be years before you know the truth if I don't tell you now since I may not return."

VieVie screamed in pain as she fell to her knees. The tears which I had pent-up for so long streamed from my downcast eyes. We both huddled him in our arms as his face quickly covered in our tears. *Are some of those his tears?* It appeared so.

"Now, VieVie, this is not the time. I have told you over and over this may happen. Remember our discussion about how you need to be strong and persevere? I want you to contact Cécile at some point. Do you hear me? When things become unbearable or before, you must contact *her*." VieVie slipped into "her" world as often occurred when life became too much.

"Good, Mark, I'm glad she is safe in 'her' world. Listen carefully to me. Your parents left your home. The Nazis transported them with hundreds of others to a concentration camp. At this point, we do not know the exact location of where they may be."

His news was all too much. From the moment I walked into this room tonight, the General told me nothing but bad news. I heard myself crying but felt nothing. Was this what VieVie experienced? Did the first world war create minds which cut the life out when it became too painful? What would happen to us as preparations began for another one?

VieVie and I now listened to the news each night. By the beginning of 1939, it was clear to Parisians, another battle waited, but we continued our shielded life in denial for yet a while longer.

Most of Paris began to now shake like combat soldiers as we waited for the inevitable. No longer did we drink the hours away. Quickly, churches filled as people kneeled in prayer for the safety of their country and those whom they loved. No longer did we reference Paris as "The City of Light" maybe of "Doubt and Doom."

"Mark, listen to me. You must become a man now, right now, at this moment! Do you hear me? What waits for you and VieVie and all

Parisians is not pretty. You must become serious with life. I am rushing to what we think will be our frontline. If things get bad, contact Cécile. Do you understand? She has many connected friends. Don't forget. There is much to tell you, but my mind contains more than I can process. It seems there was another item of importance to discuss, but I am overwhelmed and unable to remember everything at the moment. We should have had this discussion earlier but I could not. I forget much of importance, but for some reason, I think of Cécile. You must find her."

"I know why. Cécile was your lover. You must be concerned with her safety."

"Ah, Mark, Cécile was more than my lover. She is the bravest woman whom I have ever known. Don't forget to find her if you are in danger. Maybe, it is better I leave now. I no longer hunger. I love you, Mark. I leave all I love in your hands."

Sadly, he looked at his wife. His bags waited next to the door. Anne-Laure came into the room dabbing her eyes. The two looked sadly at each other, he waved to her, with a look of foreboding. He was gone.

CHAPTER TEN

PREPARATIONS FOR WAR

As early as the spring of 1939, war with Germany already seemed inevitable. Parisians began the first defense exercise which took place on 2 February, as city workers started digging twenty kilometers of trenches. Soon, these surrounded the city squares and parks. Their use was for bomb shelters.

On 10 March 1939, the first gas masks were issued to the civil population of Paris. All over the city, signs were posted showing the location of bomb shelters in case of future air raids. No longer did time drag past us. Events now seemed to happen too quickly. All of this was surreal, preposterous.

Am I about to die? Are my parents already gone? Carefully, I studied my new surroundings. My mind was a jumble of fear, sadness and indescribable joy. Finally, I had received the life of my dreams but at what cost?

If I must die, maybe to die in my home surrounded by people who knew me well and loved me would be more desirable? As other Parisians left in fear, I treasured my new home. Of course, I had no idea of the preparations underway for the waiting destruction. My feelings of elation at escaping Germany were new. How could I allow the adverse actions of the coming war to strip me of my newfound joy? I was still unaware of how frightening things were becoming around me. It seemed impossible a war could occur. I, like so many others, now lived in uncontrollable denial. The easiest way of coping was to pretend things were as usual.

I concentrated on my exciting, new world. The need to go shopping soon, I added to my empty list of "future activities." Of course, I knew something dire waited, but there was no way to plan for it. Instead, I merely tried to live as though life was sane.

47

"Mark, there is no news of the General. My husband is at the Western Front! What has become of him? I fear I am unable to endure all of this!" There was no consoling her. We heard Britain notified the French military to *resist at all costs,* but they denied us military assistance. Earlier, we had erred drastically in our assessment of Germany's military and tactical abilities. Our officials sent French forces to Belgium. There, they expected the Germans to attack. Instead, our foe advanced through the Ardennes Forest of France. What happened was a slaughter because we hadn't prepared for the forces who marched toward us.

The maniacal dictator was even allowed to invade Czechoslovakia on 15 March 1939, without any country raising a hand to stop him! All Hitler requested, our French officials reluctantly handed him without conflict. On 19 March, we noticed signs strategically posted around the city. They guided us to the nearest shelters.

It is coming! There is absolutely nothing we can do. Has the world gone insane? In June of 1939, German tanks broke through the Central Front getting closer to Paris. VieVie collapsed into a heap of tears and anger. On the late evening of 14 June 1939, we received news General La Fontaine died in battle at the French Front when the invasion started a little earlier. Personally, at that time, I was glad he avoided the horrors of what waited. VieVie's worst fears had occurred. She screamed for hours until the doctors injected her with increasing amounts of sedation. When I saw her, I cried. No longer was my Love the beauty of earlier days. Her eyes appeared hollow as the eyes of the German people in my dream. Frequently, she would point into the air and mumble incoherent phrases. Did she see the General standing in front of her reaching arms? Sometimes, she would smile sweetly, but most of the time, her face was void of any recognition of life around her. It broke my heart, but worst of all was her refusal to look at me or allow me to hug or kiss her. She hated me now because of her earlier actions behind the General's back. For me, it was hell. What was I supposed to do? How could I honor my promise to the General? *She has broken!*

On 14 July 1939, the one-hundred-fiftieth anniversary of the storming of the Bastille, British soldiers marched with French units in the national parade on the Champs-Élysées. On 25 August, the government seized copies of the communist newspapers *L'Humanité* and *Le Soir* for praising the *Hitler-Stalin Pact*. VieVie and I watched all of the news as if we observed a movie. All feeling stopped. Life became freakish.

Deterioration in our lives continued. Panic gripped Paris. The streets were empty. Earlier news, which we received about the General, devastated us in all we did. We moped. We now feared for our lives and those of our fellow Parisians.

On 23 August, the French residents received information from newspapers. The German foreign minister, Joachim von Ribbentrop, and Russian minister Vyacheslav Molotov together had signed the *Hitler-Stalin Pact of Non-Aggression. L'Humanité*, the daily newspaper of the French Communist Party (PCF), was ecstatic as they referred to Stalin as great.

Great? Stalin? General La Fontaine was great, not that murderer, Stalin. What was happening? Were they welcoming the communists into Paris? The copies of their newspaper and the other Communist newspaper, *Ce Soir*, were finally seized by the police and their publication suspended at once. We breathed a quick sigh of relief, but it was brief.

On 27 August, in anticipation of air raids, workmen had begun removing the stained glass windows of the *Sainte-Chapelle*. Curators at the Louvre, summoned back from summer vacation, aided by packers from the nearby department stores, began indexing and packing the significant works of art. Lovingly, the workers placed them inside crates labeled only with numbers to disguise their contents. Long, slow convoys of trucks, drove the art with headlights off to observe the imposed blackout, to the *châteaux of the Loire Valley* and other designated locations. Sadly, Paris watched and waited for the bombs.

On 31 August, anticipating bombardment, the French government evacuated thirty-thousand children out of their home to the *Province* (regions outside Paris). That night, the street lights were first turned off as a measure against German air raids.

Then, on 1 September 1939, Hitler did the unthinkable, he sent his armies into Poland. On that day, with the news Germany had invaded Poland, France declared a general mobilization and a *State of Siege* with war proclaimed on 3 September 1939. The Polish people refused to allow his aggression without a fight. They rose up and fought gallantly!

At the same time, Britain and France finally declared war on Germany. On the eve of World War II, Berlin's population was four million point thirty-four; this was the second largest city in Europe. For the next six years, a world war raged. More than fifty-million people would die as a consequence of a madman's revenge.

Conditions in Paris continued to worsen at an alarming pace. The hatred toward Germans and Jews inside of Paris was frightening! More and more often, I feared to leave home due to the possibility someone may question me or demand to know my relationship with the La Fontaine's. Where had the General placed my papers? Paralyzed with fear, I no longer ate nor was I able to sleep. Instead, I systematically began to search the house for my vital information. Should the French become suspicious, I was a sitting duck to any accusation because I had *nothing!* Of course, if I had my documentation, I would have been shipped to a concentration camp. If it were possible, the Jew in France soon became even more hated than the German, and I was both.

Frequently, I recalled my last hours with the General and his declaration he needed to discuss something of grave importance but was unable to remember it. Was my current problem of what he referenced? He would have told me where he hid my papers before leaving if his mind was clear. General La Fontaine was correct. I should have been of more help and not expected him to think of everything as he faced shipment to the Western Front. A few weeks after the demise of the General, as the maid and I searched for my passport, Anne-Laure stood loyally at my side. She now was aware of my plight. Maybe, I shouldn't have told her of my circumstances, of my race, but I felt alone and needed a friend. I think, she always knew of my predicament.

Together, we searched every day. The house was huge and old; it became impossible to check each object thoroughly. One day, as we explored, VieVie walked into the room. She had finally showered. Her golden locks were clean and shiny but pulled away from her face. Her appearance had changed drastically. Her new appearance made her look older and created a stern look. Her eyes no longer shined but remained dull and lifeless. She covered herself as I had never seen before in an old dress which was much too large for her.

Did her dress belong to the mother of the General? No longer did she find it humorous to expose her body. Still, she finally smiled at me.

"Mark, I have returned from Hell. No longer will I be the same. Life is too short. With the loss of my beloved, I understand the pain which I caused him. Never will I forgive myself. Earlier, it seemed as though life stretched before us forever. Now, I understand how fleeting it is. You are my son, as you were meant to be, *not* my lover. Please forgive me for the terrible position in which I have placed you. Yesterday, old friends of the Generals visited me. They told me it is only days before we are invaded here in Paris. The General had a plan for you; I know this. Foggily, I recall him saying he had 'new papers' drawn for you. We must find these before suspicions increase. You no longer sound German. Never did you look German as did your father. I believe you have your mother's looks so I don't think they can label you 'German' or 'Jew,' but we must find the documents. If only you and I had been more responsible, we would not be forced to live with this guilt and shame for the pain we caused my husband and your friend. Also, we would not be dealing with not knowing where Louie hid your information. Our situation is our own making. We both face deportation and maybe death."

Softly, she began to cry. I was speechless. All she stated was true. Day after day, hour after hour, we searched. One day, as VieVie and Anne-Laure looked upstairs, I traced my entry into the house on my first day so long ago. I again entered the massive old, wooden door and walked to the table where I sat one early morning. Smiling, as I relived those days of peace and freedom, suddenly, I stood and walked toward the door where the maid had led me to my little house. As if a fog cleared from around me, I knew where my fate lied! Running toward the small green cabinet, I called for VieVie and Anne-Laure to join me in my search.

"I know! I know where he hid my things. Now, I remember his cautioning me to 'remember this cabinet.'" Pointing toward the green chest, I began to remove all of the dishes. The others helped me. Once everything had been cleared and sat on the floor, VieVie and I looked sadly at each other.

"Mark, I'm sorry. For a moment, I thought we had liberated you from certain death." Again, she began to shake and cry as though she could not bear any more pain and disappointment. Out of the blue, Anne-Laure calmly spoke.

"The hiding place. The armoire contains a hiding place. One day, long ago, as I dusted, I found it. I showed it to the General. We need a ladder." Walking away to a utility closet, she soon returned carrying a tall step stool. Quickly, I opened it and climbed to the top.

As I turned to look at the two women, who were all that remained in my life, I took a deep breath. VieVie had stopped crying. Carefully, I looked at the top of the green armoire; there was no opening. Then, with my right hand, I methodically began to feel the wood. Screaming with joy, I felt the precise incision which cut into the cabinet. Whoever did this had done so with great skill. Perhaps as a hiding place during the first war?

"Anne-Laure, quickly, get me a sharp object so I can pry this open." Soon, the maid returned with a small knife. As I caught the tip of a corner with the blade, I could feel resistance. Slowly, I continued to lift the top as the women stood breathlessly around my feet. To my amazement, inside of the small space of about two feet, carefully folded was my new identity. Beneath it was the papers which might have sent me to my death. I held them both into the air with tears of joy! VieVie again crumbled to the floor. At least, we now had a chance! With haste, I ran to my little house to hide them in a place only I knew. The sobs of my dear, little love followed me.

Thank you, my dear friend for your love and concern for me, a traitor to you!

CHAPTER ELEVEN

VICTOR LA FONTAINE

Not only had the General spared my life with a new identity, but he also wrote a beautiful letter of love to VieVie and me which he hid inside of the armoire. With great consideration, VieVie's husband revealed he had been acutely aware of the affair which existed not so hidden from him. Obviously, he did know, but according to him, so did "most of Paris." Although he over-stated his concept, he then detailed his adoration for both of us. We cried tears of relief. We must carry our deceitful actions and the pain which we inflicted on someone whom we both loved due to our lustful natures; the General explained he understood and forgave us. He went on to say we needed to reference my identity as his brother's son. Louie did have a nephew named Victor whose name I now carried. Victor had gone missing. They never discovered his body. His demise occurred many years earlier. The incident dealt great pain to the La Fontaine family.

"Yes, I remember this time. It was right after our wedding. The entire family appeared to love Victor so much. Louie stated once, he believed one of his reasons for easily loving you was due to your resemblance to his nephew. I guess if anyone questions us, we have good reason to be confident they can't prove otherwise. We are saved! Our beloved General has saved both of us yet *again*."

It wasn't clear to me why she said, "Again" but later, I discovered VieVie had attempted suicide after Hans left her. The General had nursed her to as much wellness as she would obtain from her mental brokenness. He loved her and brought her back to enjoy life, but she was never the same. Had his current actions prevented her demise once more?

Suddenly, VieVie and I began to paint and revisit the markets together, but joy had left most Parisians. Long, sad faces peered briefly, fearfully at us in the stalls. Without discussing it, we prepared ourselves for the inevitable. On 3 of September 1939, the Germans decided to invade France. War was no longer fear; it became our reality.

Life continued to ebb as once again things slowed for us while we now waited for the inevitable. French officials began to claim Paris would receive no bombs! Destruction must be avoided!

How can this be? These German brutes will surely try to decimate Paris! Meticulously, life ebbed forward but in a surreal way. VieVie, Anne-Laure and I talked about the General fondly each evening at dinner. Suppers were no longer elaborate events but simple ones. Anne-Laure served our meals quietly. We did the unthinkable; we invited our maid to join us. Wealthy French citizens were aware the palatial homes and great assets might be a catalyst for the German's attention when they invaded us. We swapped old war stories in the streets about the barbarism of the invaders who appeared destined to occupy our beloved boulevards.

How can we save Paris from destruction? Our City officials protected the architectural landmarks of the town with sandbags. The French Army waited in the fortifications of the *Maginot Line*. Sadly, inside Paris, ration cards for gasoline were issued. We received restrictions on the sale of meat. Quietly in February 1940, ration cards for food were issued. Still, cafés and theaters continued operation for those brave enough to attend.

On 10 May 1940, when the Germans carried out air raids on Belgium and Holland, Hitler began his take-over. Next, his troops took Northern France despite massive resistance from the allied troops. By 4 June 1940, three hundred forty-thousand allied forces bravely provided relief for the British soldiers as British citizens triumphantly offered transportation back home. Ten days later, the RAF destroyed all bridges from Rouen to Mantes as they tried to stop the German advance. From 10 May 1940, for six full weeks, the German forces defeated the allies and conquered France, Belgium, Luxembourg and the Netherlands. Shortly, the Germans claimed "victory" while descending toward the "The City of Light." Without any fighting in the streets of Paris, happily, the victors approached us to claim their spoils.

Have the Germans actually honored their promises not to bomb Paris? VieVie and I discussed our situation. Time was running out for Jews expecting solace here.

"It is only a matter of time before the Germans continue to push forward even though I heard the sixty remaining French divisions continue to fight bravely. There is no way we can win against them. They are superior to us, as they swear. Now, they hammer our *Maginot Line* while they continue to collapse our army." The British General Staff implored us to defend Paris street-by-street if necessary, but Pétain scoffed at such a request.

Without our retaliation, the Germans determined to ruin France's economy and military. Without doing much to stop them, we were forced to watch as they annihilated our population. They crippled our morale while reducing our ability to aide other occupied nations. Without regard to the losses we suffered, the Germans *did* bomb Paris while not caring those who died were mostly civilians, including school children. Yes, they had created havoc and terror in our very soul. Town officials wanted to flee, who could blame them? Instead, France's Minister Of The Interior prevented such action by threatening them with severe penalties should they attempt to leave.

As French citizens, we had done as instructed after we received information there would be no bombs, but on 3 June, on this day in 1940, the German Air Force bombed Paris. As we suffered in horror, two hundred fifty-four innocents died, most of them civilians. The lies and treachery had begun. They accomplished their purpose. We feared them, but we hated them more.

Later, we learned the French leaders, as early as 6 June 1940, decided to surrender Paris and declare it an "open city." Our leader, Petain, had done this! Although this action was unpopular, General Hering, France's military governor, made the decision. The bombing which we received was bad enough, but these brutes could have destroyed us. No one wanted to witness the destruction of Paris, so they gave it away.

On 8 June, we heard the sound of distant artillery fire in our beloved Paris. Desperate refugees managed to depart *Gare d'Austerlitz* without knowing of their destination. Then on 10 June, the French government finally did leave Paris, first to *Tours* and then to *Bordeaux*. At this point, thousands of Parisians followed them. VieVie and I stood in the street watching this slow-moving river of refugees as they exited the city in automobiles, tourist buses, trucks, wagons, carts, bicycles and on foot. One of our friends announced it took ten hours to cover thirty kilometers. Still, VieVie and I watched. Shortly after the wealthier arrondissements of the city appeared nearly deserted. Our Parisian working class of the 14th arrondissement dropped from one hundred seventy-eight thousand to forty-nine thousand, but my love and I refused to abandon our beloved Paris.

Shock swept over us when on the tenth day of June, the French government declared Paris "an open city." The German 18th Army deployed against us in Paris. Our soldiers resisted bravely, but their line fell. So it was, at 5:30 on the morning of 14 June, the first German soldiers entered our city at *Porte de La Villette* and took the *rue de Flandres* as they marched in formation toward the center. Several German columns followed them while they moved to the key intersections. Finally, German military vehicles rolled down our streets with loudspeakers. These hideous vehicles drove among us instructing Parisians not to leave their buildings. At eight in the morning, their German officers arrived at the *Invalides*, the new headquarters of our military governor of Paris, Henri Dentz. Joyfully, they continued until arriving at the *Prefecture of Police*. Sadly, the *Prefect*, Roger Langeron, waited for whatever would follow.

The Germans kindly "invited" the French officials to receive their German captors. We couldn't help but witness as much of this as possible as Parisians watched from balconies and windows while the Germans proudly hung a swastika flag at the *Arc de Triomphe*, but these actions weren't enough. Soon, the occupiers organized military parades accompanied by a marching band on the *Champs Élysées* and *Avenue Foch*. Their "little march" wasn't for the benefit of Paris but primarily for the benefit of the German army photographers and newsreel cameramen.

While this debauchery occurred, the French Prime Minister, Paul Reynaud, dismissed his Commander, Maurice Gamelin. As planned, he filled the Commander's position with the seventy-three-year-old Maxime Weygand. Reynaud also named the eighty-four-year-old Philippe Pétain, who had been a great hero of the First World War, as Deputy Prime Minister. Neither man thought victory existed for France, so they determined to prevent the destruction of Paris.

Although at this time, the British Expeditionary Force completed its evacuation at Dunkirk and France, they teetered on the edge of collapse to our German invaders. The British War Cabinet received news Norway's king, Haakon, confidently predicted the allies would win this world war in the end. After his statement, he left Norway for England while his own country was left to suffer under German occupation. So it was hell descended upon us. We watched as many citizens made loud proclamations of love and loyalty to France only to run with their heads down for safety. The average citizen had nowhere to run. Still, VieVie and I remained loyal to the city we loved so much.

"How bad can this occupation be? Think about it. If we 'sweat it out, lay low' as the General liked to say, 'don't call attention.' What can they do to us?" Our naivety came from fear and denial. I was a Jew.

Where can I go? VieVie could have left without any problem, but I was too afraid to attempt running again. My love was true to her earlier proclamation of love; she never left me.

When the Germans occupied Paris, two-thirds of our residents, particularly those in the wealthier neighborhoods, escaped to the countryside. Their quick exodus was known as the *Exode de 1940.* Masses of people from the Netherlands, Belgium, Luxembourg, the North and east of France fled after the German victory of the *Battle of Sedan.* Silently, we watched exodus after exodus file down our streets. I touched the hand of the woman who could have saved herself but stood with a man filled with fear.

On the early morning of 14 June 1940, Parisians awakened to bullhorns yelling in a foreign language. The Germans entered as the French troops withdrew without a struggle. We did as instructed so a violent battle would not destroy Paris. Both sides of Germany and France finally had reached a peaceful surrender. It was a somber day for us to witness our proud country fall into the hands of these monsters while there appeared no resistance to their invasion. Troops advanced from the Northeast to the Northwest, past the *Arc De Triomphe,* down the *Champs Elysees,* to the *Place de la Concorde.* We watched in horror as if we were small children. There was no comfort anywhere in the land. VieVie cried. I realized that I had signed our death certificates. Such a foolish and fearful man as I would have disappointed the great General whom I admired more than any other person alive.

The cost of war and her many losses now marked VieVie's face with lines but not so deeply as most. Her golden hair appeared even whiter as the process of aging crept speedily upon her. Her silver threaded hair now did not shine so brilliantly. Those full, pink lips withered a little and looked thin and cracked. The shine returned to eyes of blue somewhat, but nothing like in her younger days. My VieVie was now an aged lady but remained beautiful to me. *When did this happen? How did we become this elderly?*

Also, at this time, on the evening of 16 June 1940, Prime Minister Reynaud resigned. On the morning of 17 June, General de Gaulle left *Bordeaux* by plane for London. At this time, with heavy hearts around midday, we Parisians gathered around radios while we listened to Pétain, the new head of the French government, announce we must stop hostilities. He demanded all fighting against the Germans stop.

The defeatism of the Frenchman was apparent in almost every face. News spread at the lack of morale inside of France. Winston Churchill earlier had phoned Prime Minister Reynaud to offer him hope, but our PM had been inconsolable. We all were! Our officials burned French archives to prevent them from falling into prying German hands. At this point, there had been no agreement, but to our grief, the French army stopped fighting as earlier instructed.

It appears we have lost everything. Great sadness hangs heavily in our streets. On 18 June 1940, Charles de Gaulle, an obscure French Brigadier General, addressed the people of France from London on the BBC. He requested the French *continue* to battle against the German aggressors. Although few heard his broadcast at the time, afterward, it did receive publication. His speech stirred those in occupied France but initially appeared less well received in Vichy France. Still, French people governed that area, so his passionate speech must have moved their souls! Then, the Vichy government became blatant as they began to collaborate openly with the Germans. They had crossed the line!

VieVie and I wept when we heard the news on 22 June 1940, the *Second Armistice at Compiègne* received signatures by French and German officials. This action divided France into a neutral Vichy régime led by General Marshal Philippe Pétain who was a hero from the earlier world war. Now, his régime superseded the *Third Republic* as he bowed to German occupation. Italy took a small occupied zone in our southeast or Vichy régime which controlled the unoccupied south or *Zone Libre*. This division of our treasured Parisian jewel remained in effect until November of 1942.

The German military freely assumed the seats in the most exquisite dining rooms as they also did in the best theaters and museums. Our leaders handed these abusers our beautiful city without a fight. On the 22 June 1940, France signed an armistice with Germany. Finally, the most hated Adolf Hitler visited Paris for the first and only time on 23 June 1940. He would never return. Most of the French harbored deep hatred toward him, but plenty supported and cheered him as they blatantly saluted him. This man, Adolf Hitler, arrived for a rapid tour by car. The German sculptor, Arno Breker, and Hitler's architect, Albert Speer, rode with him. Both of these men earlier had lived in Paris. Proudly, they guided his tour. Together, they rode to the Opera House and later viewed the Eiffel Tower from the terrace of the *Palace of Chaillot*. They even stood at Napoleon's tomb. Before leaving, they visited the artist's quarter of *Montmartre* on this, Hitler's first and final visit to our city. *He can't depart soon enough!*

The day of 23 June 1940, the German occupation authorities ordered all French persons to turn in any weapons and shortwave receivers they possessed or face severe measures. Within Paris, the opposition was still isolated and slow to build. On 2 August, de Gaulle was condemned to death for treason, in absentia, by Marshal Pétain's new government. His regime had gone too far. Anger boiled in our souls. It was as if we recognized each other. There was a look in the eye as we passed on the streets.

Something is happening. A new and different energy is forming! Once the Occupation had begun, citizens who exited earlier started to return. By 7 July 1940, the city government estimated the population had risen again to one and a half million; it climbed to two million by October 22 and two and a half million by 1 January 1941. VieVie and I hugged; we agreed we had made the correct decision not to leave earlier when so many Parisians fled. Many people slowly returned to generational homes only to find them occupied by Germans. Our house remained safe and undisturbed, at least so far, because we had not left it vulnerable.

The Vichy Government Parliament met on 9 July 1940, to consider our future in Paris. Pierre Laval, who was a great hero at the time and

Pétain's Vice Premier, dominated discussions. Sadly, he enforced the Vichy régime. He seemed confident Germany *would* become the victor and would eventually control the continent. We all should follow "as lambs without a struggle." Almost single-handedly, he persuaded parliament to remove itself and the Third Republic from existence. The final vote for his plan was five hundred sixty-nine to eighty which allowed Pétain to pass a new constitution although he never completed it. However, the real pro-fascists were Jacques Doriot and Marcel Marcel Déat. They desired the model to their régime be of Hitler and Mussolini. These two men soon left Vichy and moved to Paris. There, they accepted German profits while they strutted about as heroes. *I despise the two of them.*

During the Occupation, the French Government moved to Vichy, and Germany's Third Reich flag blatantly flew over all the French government buildings. Signs in German now stood on the main boulevards, and the clocks of Paris registered Berlin time. VieVie and I walked around our city watching in horror as the Germans changed our way of life. Their military high command moved into the Majestic Hotel on *Avenue Kléber*. The *Abwehr* (German military intelligence), resided in the *Hôtel Lutetia*. Strutting proudly, the Luftwaffe (German Air Force) took over our beloved Ritz. While the *Kriegsmarine* (German Navy) joyfully moved into the *Hôtel de la Marine* on the *Place de la Concorde*. The *Carlingue*, the French auxiliary organization of the Gestapo, proudly goose-stepped into the building at 93 *rue Lauriston* while the German commandant of Paris and his staff moved into the *Hôtel Meurice* on the *rue de Rivoli*. VieVie and I could not believe two of our favorites, the Ritz and the *Hôtel Meurice*, received the German occupiers. All of this saddened us as we remembered joyful times we once had spent there.

Things continue to worsen during the fall of 1940 which marked the beginning of food rationing as we received cards which classified us according to age and food needs. *The Law of Rationing of Food:* tobacco, coal and clothing was passed later in September of 1940. Each year, we pulled our belts tighter as we lost weight due to the scarcity of necessary items. Our French press and our radios broadcasted only German propaganda. Even our listening to the BBC became unlawful. We began to feel like prisoners in our own land. *Indeed, we are prisoners!*

We didn't need to search far to find a way to redemption. Soon, we heard of a group called the *Resistance Organization* in Paris. It formed in September 1940 by a group of scholars connected with the *Musée de l'Homme*, the ethnology museum located at the *Palais de Chaillot*.

We now had our champions as the Occupation, by Paris students, took place on 11 November 1940. This date was the anniversary of the end of the First World War. Yes, the new war continued, but anti-German clandestine groups and networks now evolved. Our Resistance had not yet received unification. No, not yet, as some of our team pledged loyalty to the French Communist Party and others to General Charles de Gaulle in London. These brave patriots wrote slogans on walls and organized an underground press. As time passed, we heard of attacks on German officers. Reprisals by the Germans to these youth were swift and harsh

On a day, which usually featured patriotic ceremonies of remembrance, our hearts broke at the state of events in France on *this* beloved day, 11 November, the end of World War I. As if anticipating trouble, the German authorities banned any commemoration and made it a regular school and work day. Nonetheless, the students of Paris *lycées* (high schools) circulated handbills and leaflets calling for students to boycott classes and meet at the Tomb of the Unknown Soldier beneath the *Arc de Triomphe*. Our youth stirred us into action as is the case in many revolts. The day began quietly, as some twenty-thousand students laid wreaths and bouquets at the tomb and the statue of Georges Clemenceau, on *Place Clemenceau,* by the *Champs Élysées.* Although their actions created tension and concern, the French and German authorities tolerated them.

At midday, the demonstration became more provocative; some students carried a *floral Cross of Lorraine*, the symbol of de Gaulle's Free France. Now, their actions were becoming personal to the persons in charge who chased the students away. At nightfall, the event became more violent. These once peaceful youth now gathered, chanting *"Vive la France"* and *"Vive l'Angleterre"* while they invaded a local bar popular with the fascist youth group. At 6:00 p.m., the students began scuffling with police. Soon enough, German soldiers arrived, surrounded the young people, and closed the entrance of the metro stations. They charged at the students with fixed bayonets, firing shots in the air.

Afterward, the Vichy government announced one hundred and twenty-three arrests and one student wounded. These youth were arrested, taken to the prisons of *La Santé*, *Cherche-Midi*, and *Fresnes*. Unfortunately, once there, they were abused and left standing in the pouring rain. Soldiers threatened many of the young while they pretended to be a firing squad scaring them. These actions closed the prestigious Sorbonne University.

At the beginning of the Occupation, Germans treated the Jews in Paris with particular harshness. On 18 October 1940, the German occupiers of our country decreed what is known as the *Ordonnance d'Aryanisation*. This aggressive act barred the Jewish people from liberal professions as well as restaurants and public places. Eventually, the Nazi leaders seized their property.

On 15 December, a small group of Resisters used the museum mimeograph machine as they published *Résistance*, a four-page newspaper. This short paper gave its name to the movement while news of them quickly followed. The Russian-born (French naturalized) anthropologist Boris Vildé led this group. Their first issue boldly claimed their loyalty to France and maintaining her beliefs.

Although the metro did continue to run during early days of occupation, service was frequently interrupted. Those available cars were overcrowded. Three thousand five hundred buses previously drove down our streets in 1939, but only five hundred continued in the autumn of 1940. Bicycle-taxis, once again, became popular. Even these drivers gouged us as they charged a high tariff. About the only reliable means of transport became the old standby: bicycles, but their prices soared. A used bike cost a month's salary. Our citizens did what was needed to survive. Parisians watched as our supply of fuel dropped. Our number of automobiles declined from three hundred fifty-thousand before the war to under four thousand five-hundred.

One of our friends, who sat on the terrace of a café on the *Place de la Bourse*, counted cars which passed between noon and twelve-thirty. Shaking his head, he announced there were only three. Transportation from days-gone-by such as the horse-drawn fiacre came back. Several of the cars and trucks which did circulate used *gazogene*. This poor-quality fuel sat in a tank on the roof of the vehicle. It consisted of coal gas, or methane, which they extracted from the Paris sewers. Classy, cultured Paris smelled like a barnyard. Only Germans seemed to ride proudly down our streets in gasoline-powered cars as they arrogantly held their heads back. *You swine!*

My money situation would have become dire if not for the maddening schedule of earlier when we painted with such ferocity. It was as if we realized the possibility of a day when we would become unable to withdraw our funds. VieVie had insisted we save all of the cash from our art sales which were substantial. Thankfully, I appreciated her planning in the days once halcyon for us. Those days were long past! Dearest VieVie had given all of her profits from our art to me. She could never realize she saved me. I would never be able to thank her.

Anne-Laure stood in the lines and did her best to secure all allowed for us and our dwindling staff. Many of our workers had fled returning to their home countries. Remorsefully, we watched many people, who had worked for the General for generations, carrying their few possessions back to foreign lands. Often, we discussed Anne-Laure and the possibility she might leave us someday. What a sad thought! She had become one of us; she was family now.

Winter descended with a vengeance Christmas of 1940. The temperature in France was chilling as were the frozen souls of her people. We could not recall a more bone-freezing time in our city's history. Still, when we realized there would not be a war in the streets, people wanted to go outdoors and feel alive again. Many slid down the slopes of *Montmartre*. These freezing conditions only exacerbated the shortage of coal and warmth in our homes. The only way to purchase this gift of heat was on the black market. People huddled together for warmth. More babies were born as couples attempted not to freeze. There was no meat available for most of us. The French citizens received little bread as the nutritional value of our diets crashed. Movies were a draw for many as we sat in theaters close to our captors.

For us Parisians, the Occupation dealt us a series of frustrations. It seemed everyone suffered shortages and humiliations. Soon, the Germans placed a curfew on us from nine in the evening until five in the morning. Nights in Paris found a dark and haunting city as all went black. If one was brave enough to venture out, figures could be seen scurrying about within the charcoal shadows, they passed. Who were those brave souls and what did they do as they broke laws which most of us fearfully obeyed?

Sadly, we watched as our militia, police and internal security, which had been organized by the French, committed themselves to the Gestapo. They positioned themselves against the Jews, communists and the beginning of the Resistance Fighters. How could they support our invaders? Once again, their actions made no sense to most of us. The aforementioned targeted people were now believed to be the enemy by many Frenchmen. Nasty, vicious propaganda spread over Paris which attacked residents who had resided here since their birth. The French Resistance began to rise more dramatically at this time. There appeared to be two types of Resistance fighters. There were those who provided an essential role by gleaning information, and those who fought. Both were vital to the success of the movement. Personally, I believed our liberation depended on these gallant members.

Many Parisians weren't aware of the support we had from our allies and the selfless way they fought to free us. VieVie and I wished we knew these gallant fighters. They became a beacon of hope to us.

Quietly, the people in the house of General La Fontaine existed in life. We merely existed. Maybe, there wasn't terrible destruction for us as we earlier feared, but something as horrible *was* happening. Innocent Jews were rounded up and forced into concentration camps. I may be walking down the street with VieVie when soldiers passed shoving me out of the way. Frequently, I turned to witness yelling, angry soldiers pushing innocent people into lines. Even the children cried as they stood for hours with their families waiting for a fate which remained unclear. It was impossible not to cry as we looked into eyes of fear and confusion. *What have they done to deserve this?*

I could tell from the pain on their faces; these innocents had already suffered as they had hidden for months in attics and basements. Guilt assailed me. I was one of *them*, Jewish. It was I who should have stood by their side as I should have faced the draft back in Germany. Fearfully, I watched as Nazis herded these dejected families like cattle onto trains. Looking into hollow eyes of fear, my dream, on such a bright day when Paris was indeed the City of Light, stole into my captive mind. My body became racked with guilt for the way I treated my parents as well as the General, and now, I was a fraud and a liar. Could I ever believe myself to be anything of value? I doubted it. VieVie cried all of the time as we witnessed such inhumanity. No longer were we golden. We were as cowardly as anyone. Maybe, we were safe to live our shallow lives, but our minds contained deep scars of shame.

"Mark, we must do something to help them."

"What do you suggest? Do *you* want to die? If you do, everything your husband fought so gallantly to save, we lose. Do you want that to happen?" Frequently, we argued.

For all of 1940, the German military occupied Northern France. The Vichy régime governed as a nominal governor for that area. It was a de facto capital. France was declared, "Vichy," for two hundred and twenty miles to the South. Germans strutted around as victors which they were for a while. The French Vichy government never joined the Axis allies while the French police ordered Jews and "other undesirables" such as communists and political refugees imprisoned. Surprisingly, many of the French residents supported such actions to keep the autonomy and the integrity of their country.

The feeling of the Parisians toward our occupiers varied considerably. Some Parisians saw the Germans as an accessible source of money; others, as the *Prefect of the Seine*. Roger Langeron (arrested on 23 June 1940) could not even see them. It was as if they were "transparent" he had stated. It was a little hard for most of us "not see them." The attitude of members of the French Communist Party was complicated. The Party had long denounced Nazism and Fascism, but after the signing of the *Molotov–Ribbentrop Pact* on 23 August 1939, they had to reverse their direction. The editors of the Communist Party newspaper, *L'Humanité*, which had been closed down by the French government, asked the Germans for permission to resume publishing. The paper was allowed to reopen.

The Party also requested workers return to their positions in the armaments factories which were now producing for the Germans. Many individual communists opposed the Nazis, but the ambivalent official attitude of the Party only lasted until *Operation Barbarossa*, the German attack on the Soviet Union on 22 June 1941.

"Mark, I can't do this any longer. Standing idly by as innocent families are slaughtered. It is impossible for me to live like this. How can we watch friends, who fight for our liberation, our French friends, suffer at the hands of barbarians? I have decided no longer shall I live a futile and shallow life. The first thing I want to change is my name. There will be other alterations to my life. No longer will I be called VieVie which sounds youthful. No longer can I make that claim. I am old beyond my years. My life has been full and filled with happiness. Three men have deeply adored me. If I die tomorrow, I can truly say my life has been happy but has it accomplished anything? No, this will change as I change my name. I must help stop this madness."

VieVie asked me to call her forever after "Genny" which I obediently did. No longer did we sleep together or behave like a couple in love. With the death of our beloved General, all of the passion and lust also died. Life and death flowed in the streets of Paris each day. If you hid your identity, as I did, caution and daily appearances mattered. For all practical purposes, we were an aunt with her beloved nephew. Our relationship was nothing more nor less in actuality.

Apparently, the French Resistance began as two significant symbols of the movement surfaced. They were General Leclerc and Jean Moulin. At the same time, the Vichy France stood with confusion to the citizens of our country. We found it difficult to understand their goals and how they functioned. Each day, it seemed there were new restrictions or groups claiming relevance. Philippe Pétain headed this mostly despised Vichy regime. He represented the "Free Zone" in Southern metropolitan France. Genny and I tried to understand how the Germans could be given such freedom as they had their private area.

Most of us hated what Pétain represented. All of this insanity created considerable confusion and even embarrassment for our citizens. The Americans, Canadians, British and Senegalese fought for our freedom as did many French soldiers, but the sting was we had to hand our beloved city over on a platter even though the brutes had spared our destruction. It was difficult to explain the Vichy State as we all tried to make sense of it. At the time, it appeared we didn't question the arrangement, but underneath that apparently peaceful acceptance, there raged a lion of unexpected ferociousness. It rose silently but angrily within our darkened streets. Soon, the French Resistance made us all proud as much as the Vichy régime created shame.

CHAPTER TWELVE

THE VICHY STATE

"Genny, it feels as though we are all traitors to Paris!" I shouted one early morning at breakfast.

Nothing surprised Genny and me any longer. On 10 January 1941, we walked down a street of our beloved Paris for a brief stroll and fresh air. German soldiers pushed us into a nearby wall as they paraded a Jewish family past. My heart broke. Looking into their faces, I could only remember my dream so long ago. Bile filled my throat. Why did these evil thugs think they could continue harming innocents? It made me angry and physically ill. I looked into the downcast faces of that little family with dread. There was no emotion in their eyes. After months of hiding while they continuously lived in terror, now their time was up! The German thugs prevailed! I wondered how many of the onlookers around us were like me? How many German-Jews had received help from brave souls who risked their lives to stand up to the inhuman actions of these brainwashed robots? Also, how many French families hid those of the Jewish descent? *Can these Germans sleep at night?*

On the street, we heard horrible tales which seemed impossible to believe. Denial was the only way to exist. *When will they discover me?* It was only a matter of time. Genny and I never discussed my situation, but it was at the forefront of our minds. Would Anne-Laure squeal on me? Such occurrences happened more and more as beloved household help sought the rewards offered and the benefits supplied from Germans for pointing out their employers who harbored "undesirables" or supported French Resistance fighters such as Genny did for me.

Sometimes, I heard of French citizens who broke down and could no longer cope with life. Such actions only added to the heavy burden of family members already facing more pain and demands than they could bear. The question was, "How much worse can it get?"

"Did you see the little girl's face? I thought about running to her and grabbing her from the clutches of those idiots!"

"And what good would that do? Then they would question us. Those same barbaric brutes would enter *our* house. Perhaps, they would confiscate your beautiful home and throw us onto the street? You know they can do anything. Would they threaten Anne-Laure until she supplied the truth about me? There are no rules, not anymore. I do understand why certain leaders established this new government, but we all realize we played right into the hands of the Germans. Sure, we spared Paris destruction but imagine the soldiers in the *Forest of Ardennes* and along the *Somme Valley* as the Germans surrounded them and those of the British and Belgian forces. What about the valor of locals at *Operation Dynamo?* Can their bravery ever be forgotten? How do you think I feel, as a man, while I let you harbor me knowing at any moment, the German officials may find us and send us to a concentration camp? Maybe, I will see my parents there. When I look into eyes like those, it is more than I can take."

We stood together by the wall and whispered. I noticed Genny's hands were shaking. Together, Genny and I watched as the small family of cultured, peaceful souls faced the hands of out of control tyranny. Although earlier, we had enjoyed the lovely spring morning, without a word, we turned and started to walk toward home.

"Hey, you! You, there, with the beautiful woman, what do you think we should do with these despicable people? You know they are Jews, right? The lowest of low forms. What do you suggest we do to them? What good are they, right?"

Everyone around looked at me. Would I be brave and answer from the heart? A giant German soldier stood with his legs spread widely apart in the warm air. The sky was a little cloudy, but on the horizon, dark clouds gathered.

Well, this is it! I'm coming, MaMa and PaPa. My breathing became labored as perspiration gathered on my face. My hands began to shake visibly. Looking into the wide eyes of the beautiful wee girl, I could not believe my words as her tears dripped onto dirty little cheeks, my utterance shattered me. The vile statement which I spoke sickened me.

"Jews? You know what needs doing, right? Do it!" I turned and walked away as my love remained on the spot. When I arrived back at the mansion, I went to my little house. Kneeling by my bed, I broke. Hysterically, I cried once more until there was nothing left. Darkness surrounded my home. I decided I would never face the woman I loved again. A little later, the door gently opened into my room. She walked toward me and kneeled beside me.

"Well, one of our fears is relieved. Anne-Laure left a note for us. She has gone back to her home, wherever that is. You know, the General hired her long before I came. I believe she worked for his parents."

In the semi-darkness, I could see Genny's hand motion into the charcoal-colored air. "My love, we must take care of ourselves, now, after all of the staff has run from Paris. You know, we could also leave. Together, we have plenty of money. Hidden money which will allow us to escape from all of this. Do you want to leave, my love? Mark, it may be difficult but possible. We do have connections because of the General."

Her voice was gentle, almost a whisper. When she spoke, "My love," I began to cry very softly. Realizing the humiliation which I suffered paled in comparison to others around us, I felt even more dejected.

"My darling, what is the point? Where would we go? We should stay here and wait. Both of us are aware of what will come for us. After the armistice presented to our leaders on 18 June, France has finally surrendered. It is over. I am sickened by the Vichy régime. In fact, I am sickened by myself and all of the others who stood cowardly by my side as we sent the small family to 'that object' in my dream."

Much earlier, I had confided my dream to Genny. It pleased me she did not try to console me by telling me anyone would have done the same thing I just did.

"Surely, in all of France, there is something we can do. There has to be a way we can fight. No longer can I stand by and witness atrocities such as today. I feel helpless." Now, I said those words! Something stood up mightily inside me. If I was to continue living, then I must resist what I witnessed today. In the uninterrupted darkness, I felt a small hand touch my right arm.

Genny is with me. Others must exist who feel as we do. How did we discover fighters in our country of lovers? Undoubtedly, we must find a way. On that evening, I began to dream of a group of warriors who would be willing to die rather than turn everything over to this group of hypocrites.

We have to find them! Clutching our brave proclamation to our chests, slowly, we began to search for a group of liberators. Daily, we carefully gleaned tidbits of news in the streets. We started hearing rumors of such an organization. Bravely, this small group collected information and established a network to help escaped French POWs as the soldiers attempted to flee the country. These early Resistance Fighters never were experienced conspirators. Sadly, this initial group was discovered and arrested in January 1941, but the word was finally out! Now, people like Genny and I knew there was a possibility of union together, at last, to fight for our freedom. Hope had not deserted us but merely slept to release a giant. A giant of hope which longed to free our beautiful jewel of Paris.

She is not dead, only sleeping. Quietly, *she* had rested in her lair until she achieved the much-needed unity.

The French produced only about two percent who became involved in Resistance activity compared with one percent of citizens who actively collaborated with the Germans. The remainder of our country, "Kept their heads down and waited for liberation to arrive." Genny and I chose to resist and resist we finally did at last!

News of this group charged those of us with a dream. Our dream of liberating Paris and ultimately all of France did not perish. There was a group of our people who rose up unafraid of treason or death from this group of foreign inhabiters. Finally, we received a gift. The gift of hope sprang eternally but silently as it raged in the dark streets of Paris. Now, we searched for each other in the darkened streets with one goal.

Liberation of Paris! Vive la Paris! If this required our very lives, so be it! Each of us prepared in our way for death. In many ways, death appeared desirable if we must be forced to live in fear as before. Genny and I had a plan but how did we implement it?

CHAPTER THIRTEEN

THE FRENCH FIGHTERS

Germany invaded the Soviet Union in June of 1941. As the Germans attacked Russia – *Operation Barbarossa* – French communists committed themselves to the Resistance movement in Paris. Politics no longer seemed relevant to the people of Paris; we wanted the Germans driven out. The French communists were accepted and gained a reputation for being aggressive Resistance Fighters. Many French people joined the movement as support for the Vichy Regime quickly waned. What a great relief to most residents of the country as we realized all was not lost!

The Resistance Movement helped in many ways. They provided the allies with intelligence, they also attacked the Germans when possible, and aided the allied airmen. Documents were passed quickly and efficiently in the streets containing the real news of our fight. After the surrender of France in June of 1940, our country went into shock and shame. Anger also flooded us. Our leaders had "sold us out!" The speed and severity of *Blitzkrieg*, a method of warfare used by the Germans, created a need to protect ourselves since our officials appeared incapable. Pétain's reputation remained highly regarded in the early days of Vichy. His leadership gave the new government some stability at least for a short time. Therefore, there was no immediate drive to create a resistance movement en masse in central and Southern France. That feeling did not last long.

There is something in our very souls which demands retaliation! Many resistance movements existed, but we did not realize the number until the word began to spread. Each had a purpose. All were vital. By the end of 1940, six underground newspapers started distribution in the North. May 1941, the first SOE agent (Special Operations Executive, a British World War II Organization) was dropped into Northern France to assist the work of the Resistance. Now, the battle began! On 22 June

1941, all the communist Resistance parties within France joined forces to create one group which gave them increased strength and solidarity.

Out of nowhere, reports came there were brave attacks by Frenchmen all over the country on German soldiers. Posters hung around our streets announcing the Germans would begin taking hostages in retaliation for these attacks. The date was 21 August 1941. However, their threats did little to slow our Resistance.

The Resistance world continued to spiral in separation from our country's new fundamental beliefs. On 2 September 1941, all Paris magistrates were asked to take an oath of allegiance to Marshal Pétain. Only one brave soul, Paul Didier, refused. The *Document of Surrender* hung on a wall in the occupied zone inside Paris directly under German authority. In just a simple sheet of paper, we were invited to surrender to our invaders without lifting a hand. *Invite indeed!*

Most of us were shocked when many French citizens collaborated with the Government of Marshal Pétain and ultimately with the Germans. We watched as they began assisting inside the city administration, the police and other government functions. Our officials must collaborate or lose their jobs. It appeared they had little choice.

The start of the Resistance by ordinary Parisians was symbolic. It was encouraged by the BBC as students scribbled the letter "V" for Victory all over Paris. At once, the Germans placed huge Vs. as symbols of their victories, on the Eiffel Tower and the National Assembly, but they couldn't stop us now! Even though the Germans controlled our newspapers, they were unable to prevent the spread of news of this bold and brave group whom we prayed would help with our freedom.

My thoughts returned to dear Hans and Abi. The same thing happened to them inside of Germany before they were loaded like cattle onto trains and sent to concentration camps. There had been no further word of their fate, but after witnessing the barbarism of these German soldiers, it wasn't difficult to imagine their future. I was one of many Parisians who feared the direction of this forced segregation.

On a bitter morning of early November 1941, I returned from standing in line for our rations. As I entered, yelling to Genny that I felt frozen, I heard a strange laugh. Even the slightest deviation from routine grabbed at my heart. Why would a stranger be here? *Can a German be inside our home?*

A little too quickly, I stomped into the bright yellow dining room. Genny claimed her usual position in the sunny window seat. Her golden hair increasingly dulled with the streaks of silver. Most all of the adults now sported such dull hair with additional silver. Most of us also lost a great deal of weight. The house was cold due to the lack of coal on this day of new beginnings. A stranger sat in my chair. She stared at me with a look of shock but soon stood and approached me.

"My goodness, Mark, how can you retain your good looks when the rest of us have faltered greatly in that department." Her voice was familiar, but who was this French woman? She appeared to be a little younger than Genny. She too remained beautiful, but deep lines crossed her brow and around her mouth.

"Surely, I haven't aged so much? Don't you recall me? It feels most strange standing in Louie's house. Mark, for goodness sake, it is I, Cécile, the General's lover."

"Oh, I have changed my name to Victor La Fontaine. My hesitation is because I haven't heard that name, Mark, in so long because I have assumed a new identity of the General's dead nephew." I blushed with embarrassment for failing to recognize the General's lover who I had met several times during his life. My gushing was the result of this embarrassment.

"You see, his memory creates deep pain for Genny and me. We regret our earlier actions."

"Mark, please, don't ever look back. To do so might mean arrest and death as you falter with feelings no longer important. Remember; you were never Mark Lichter. The only name you have ever carried is Victor La Fontaine. Such action is vital to your life, *Victor*." Two hours quickly passed as we discussed rations and how difficult it was not to enjoy a cup of coffee or a decent meal.

Softly, Cécile began to address the Resistance and their need for additional volunteers. The General's lover smiled at us frequently with a bright, contagious smile. The pretty French lady explained Genny already knew her new role in the Resistance Movement. It was one of the most dangerous jobs. The two women had talked about Madame La Fontaine's position in great detail before I arrived. I was aware Genny and I never followed the General's instructions to contact Cécile, but thankfully, she had found us.

"Genny, you must leave the room while I discuss his new role with Victor. As he will never know your assignment, you may not know his. This action is to protect both of you." The earlier Genny would have cajoled and whined as she attempted to gain information about what I would do. These actions didn't necessarily mean that she cared so much, but more a game which she always played to discover everything going on around her.

This new Genny, who immediately followed instructions, impressed me. My role was not severe or dangerous, but I faced death if they caught me participating in this group of French Resistance. Therefore, any position with this group was dangerous and potentially deadly.

"It is difficult, but remember, this will end soon. France *will* emerge united and strong with our allies, '*Vive la France* my dearest.' Also, remember we should never be seen together. Again, to do so places us all in danger. They have not marked me yet, but it will happen soon!"

Genny entered the room again with a look of sadness when my discussion, which did not last long, ended with Cécile. "Cécile, how can you be cheerful? We are all distraught with many miserable feelings. Genny and I seldom smile. Doing so is impossible. Our feelings are death waits around each corner."

"You, my friends, are over thinking all of this. Just 'keep the faith!' I hope our eyes never see each other again or it *will* be at our end. Thank you for your service." Cécile quickly pulled a light hood over her head and left. As I watched her walk down the street, she seemed to disappear into the air.

"Well, that sure explains a great many things. I like Cécile; I mean definitely like her. So, this is why the General encouraged us to find her? He wanted us to fight with the Resistance!"

Turning, I faced VieVie/Genny who sadly nodded. Then, she went into "her world." That place which I could vaguely feel from my own pain. Without a sound, I tiptoed back to my little house. I entered my main sitting room as I thought of the General. Yes, thinking of him had sent my love to her near catatonic state many times. She missed him. I knew. Seldom did we speak of him any longer, to do so caused great sadness.

How could I be this blessed? First, my parents, then the General as they each tried to provide for me. Now, it was my turn to give back to this country and these people who embraced me and provided shelter from the German monsters whom I deeply despised. It was painful to be a German as I observed their shameless actions on the streets of Paris. I dreamed someday; I would find *my* place. A country which did not ridicule and shame me for being Jewish but would welcome me with open arms. Until such a time, I would help the citizens of France. If necessary, I would give my life for them even though a segment of them continued to harbor hate and refused acceptance of my people. I was learning to be Jewish meant being rejected.

Next, I turned my attention to locating the French Resistance Headquarters. It did not seem to exist, at least not formally. Asking anyone about them may result in arrest. Genny finally ran into an old friend. Michelle was another model whom Genny once adored. They worked together years earlier. Entirely out of the blue, Michelle confided she was a Resistance Fighter. Her role was insignificant, at least to her. Was any position which resulted in death if discovered insignificant? I doubted it.

Out of nowhere, news traveled in the streets of Paris; there was a brave new organization of young people secretly fighting to aide our beleaguered country. They organized escape lines for POWs or downed allied pilots, sending intelligence about German forces to the allies by a radio transmitter. Proudly, they published and distributed flyers and newspapers to counter both Vichy and German propaganda.

Their actions were fraught with danger. *The Musée de l'Homme Group*, which was the beginning of our opposition, unfortunately, was infiltrated by a traitor. Most of that earlier team were rounded up early in 1941. The Nazis later killed seven of them. A piece of all of those who dreamed of a free Paris died as we witnessed our world continue to change. One day, there was encouragement; the next, there was death.

All of France was now accustomed to not eating. It didn't matter if we skipped a few meals. After Cécile left, I showered without eating and retired to read a little. Cécile's words deeply moved me. As I contemplated her bravery and spirit, for the first time in years, I remembered happiness. No longer would I mope around bemoaning my lack of concern for my parents or betrayal to the General. Instead,

I would focus on doing *something*. The next time I witnessed blatant abuse by the German soldiers, okay, I couldn't stand up to them on the spot, but a day was coming when I *would* act. On that day, all hell would descend against these maniacal maniacs. *Just you wait, you evil bastards!*

Entering the "big" house, a little later than usual the next morning, it was unclear what waited for me. *Has Genny recovered from her slip into a severely troubled state?*

"Good morning, my darling, you are late this morning. I figured you might be trying to decipher the words of our guest yesterday. Her visit made all things clear to me. I can go forward now without so much uncertainty and doubt. Victor, we can accomplish great things." Grabbing the slender woman, I spun her around several times before she kissed me passionately on the lips. We had not felt human in a very long time. Quickly, I stood her on the floor and walked to the table. I smiled.

"As much as I would love to continue past actions, we both know our agreement and the pain we suffered because of them. Now, we have a purpose. A noble and glorious one which we must not taint. Never again will I taste those luscious lips or hold that enticing body next to mine. Right?"

I believe a part of me wanted her to convince me of my madness. Finally, for the first time since the death of the General, I felt a sense of my manhood. It felt wonderfully ordinary to experience these feelings. I longed to carry her to the bed which she once shared with her husband, but I would not. My loved one sadly nodded her head.

"You are right. The Germans would add that to the list of indictments against us if they catch us. When they read to the crowds, your 'aunt' seduced you; I think there would be little support to help me." We both laughed. As the morning ticked past, we lounged for hours in the sunshine of the treasured window of the kitchen. No longer did our time appear chaotic or rushed. Yes, we both now recognized what we needed to do.

"Well, we can't just sit here."

"I know, but I hate to leave. Cécile instructed me my 'instrument of destruction' for the Germans would arrive soon." After a little persuasion, she agreed not to leave the house. For the remainder of the day, we painted in her studio. No words did we share. We both dreamed of accomplishing something great in our new roles of the Resistance against the Nazis.

As darkness descended over the streets of Paris, each of us continued to stroke heavy layers of oil paint over our canvas. Eventually, my fellow artist put her brushes into a small, blue, porcelain pot of paint thinner. I smiled at her.

A large group of yelling, brave Frenchmen carry me on their shoulders. They too fought for the release of France, but I am heroic! Never will I be forgotten as monuments will attest all over France. Genny slipped from the room without disrupting my thoughts. Soon, she returned carrying two glasses and a bottle.

"How about a martini? Soldiers need to unwind, you know?" Ages had passed since we shared a cocktail. I couldn't remember the last one.

"Where did you get that? I assumed there wasn't any liquor left in the house."

"Oh, it's here, but Anne-Laure and I hid it in a very safe place in case the bullies ramshackle us." The little beauty smiled with a smile which beguiled many men. What was it about her which reminded me of a young girl when she was older than me?

CHAPTER FOURTEEN
OUR NEW LIVES

All Saturday, my beauty behaved strangely. In the past, if it were a vital evening, early that morning, she would place cucumber slices on her eyes. That's what she did on this morning. Then, she gave herself a manicure and pedicure with apparent satisfaction. I had no idea what all this meant but knew something was up. Certainly, all of this represented a "big" evening ahead, but I realized if I asked her, she would laugh at me. Genny hated questions of any sort. She considered herself "a free spirit" which meant, I guess, she did not like to explain her actions. So, I decided to wait.

Acting very mysteriously, she did not come into my presence for the remainder of the day. *What is up with her?*

Hesitantly, I knocked on her door. "Cherie, what would you like for dinner?"

We didn't have many choices for dinner due to our rationed status. I heard Genny moving around inside her room. "Genny, what would you like to eat?"

I yelled the question. Again, I asked my question with great curiosity. *Something is up with Genny.*

"Oh, didn't I tell you? I have plans. You will have to dine alone tonight, my love."

"Okay. This situation is not a problem. I hope you have a nice time."

"I shall. Don't wait up for me." She giggled like a schoolgirl.

Ah, this is the way of our future since becoming Resistance Fighters? I didn't like it. I decided to stay in the main house so I could figure out her plans. The late afternoon shadows caused me a little pain. In the past, this was always our favorite time of the day. Sadly, I recalled when the house filled with music, laughter and flowers as we enjoyed too many cocktails before leaving for dinner in a seductive and alluring location.

At the time, I thought those halcyon days would last forever. Briefly, I couldn't help but remember the General and his contagious smile. Now, although it remained beautiful, the house appeared sad, lonely. Just the way I was feeling. Not knowing what to do with myself, I grabbed a book from the General's collection. Time always flew when I enjoyed a good book. Instead, the hours slowly passed before I felt hunger pains draw me back to the present. Closing my book, I yawned. As I lifted my eyes, an apparition stood before me. Confusedly, I shook my head to remove the jumbled webs.

Standing before me was my beloved. Not the one of today but years ago, when VieVie radiated youthful beauty. This woman appeared years younger. The dreamy, vanilla scent of the past surrounded her in a womanly cloud of aroma. Her alabaster skin glowed once more. The bags and darkened areas under her eyes evaporated. The silver disappeared from her hair which shined again as spun gold. A new dress of black hung on her skinny frame. The entire country had lost a great deal of weight, but due to her small size, the effect on her was dramatic. Her eyes looked huge as they glowed at me from a shrunken appearance. The result was surreal. The loss of mass caused a haunting look to surround her. This figure looked as if she may break if touched. It was sad but alluring at the same time.

"VieVie is it you? Such a long time has passed since I saw you this way. Sadly, I recall yesteryear and the wonderful times which we spent together. Never would I dream we may end this way. You are as beautiful as the first time I saw you. Please tell me; you are wearing underwear though?"

Laughingly, she lifted her dress to reveal no underwear like yesterday, yesterday over ten years ago. Right at that moment, car lights flashed into the room. She pecked my cheek and ran with glee to the awaiting car. Carefully, I lifted the curtain. Sitting in the drive was a shiny, black *Bugatti. Whom does she see now?*

A pang of jealousy stabbed my heart, but I refused to acknowledge such feelings. I was a new person. After joining the Resistance, such petty feelings must disappear; our new organization forbid them.

Instead, I entered the kitchen to scrounge for food as hunger tore at my core.

I wonder what Genny will eat tonight? Maybe, she will bring a few crumbs to me? Such a possibility seemed unlikely.

"Genny, what are you doing?" I asked to the empty room as I watched the beautiful car drive away.

What is she doing? I could only hope she was confident of her actions.

CHAPTER FIFTEEN

GENNY, THE WHORE

Sleep refused me on that evening many years ago. Genny and I had entered a new phase of our lives. I missed earlier times, happier ones. Maybe, I was finally behaving responsibly, but I didn't like it. Feelings of hurt invaded my spirit. Genny was now seeing another man.

Early in the morning, the car lights once again flashed into my bedroom. Mrs. La Fontaine had stayed out all night! Such actions were dangerous and not acceptable, at least not to me. There was a curfew issued all over Paris. Gay laughter echoed from the driveway. *At least, she could have shown discretion.*

All of the neighbors would once again be huddled together. They hated VieVie and me but loved the General. Now he was dead; these people must despise us even more. I couldn't blame them. Earlier, we made a mockery of her marriage and a brave soldier who gave so much for his country. General La Fontaine was a patriot. The entire nation had adored him. His wife and I were blatant in our actions. Deep in my heart, now since I stepped away from the wiles of VieVie La Fontaine, I knew. *My girl suffers damage beyond words.* The beautiful model was insane.

I couldn't resist; carefully, I lifted the curtains. Genny stood in the doorway of her mansion against the massive door. A dark figure firmly pressed against her. They were no longer laughing but grunting and moving. Shock filled me as did indignation. Were they having sex right under my nose in the generational home of her husband or was he raping her? What pathetic creatures they appeared in this early morning until I recalled the way I groped and pressed her under the nose of the General. So gravely, in many ways, I desired to believe this was rape, but my mind realized this was consensual.

Is she so desperate for a night out and a good dinner? I feel repulsed! These lurid actions continued for a long time, maybe thirty minutes?

Finally, she pulled away from him, but he grabbed her back into his embrace. Even though shrouded in darkness, the beginning light of day allowed me to determine; he was a mountain of a man.

He is a giant! Bile filled my throat. Considering running out to rescue her, I heard her gentle laughter again. Her playful, seductive voice teased him.

"You bad boy, I must go. Now, go on home to your wife and little girl. I need to sleep. What a night! I will never forget it. What? Yes, anytime you can break away, I will be waiting to hear from you, Adieu, my Love." She blew him a kiss.

Things were now pretty clear; rape had not occurred. This disgusting action was indeed consensual. Anger flooded me once again. I thought I could kill her if I faced her at this moment. Instead, I snuggled back under the butter-colored duvet and thought of the General. Had he ever seen similar flagrant behavior from VieVie and me? We had not tried to conceal our actions early on in our relationship. That ability came with time. Did she harbor the same uncontrollable passion for this brute? Out of necessity, sleep descended peacefully over me.

Not long after entering the peace of long needed sleep, I felt someone snuggle against me. The smells of sex, not mine, made me retch. Opening my eyes, I saw the small woman, I once adored, smile at me.

"Good morning, Cherie! I missed you last night. Oh, what a night we enjoyed! My date took me to *Hôtel Meurice* on the *rue de Rivoli*. Our meal was delicious. You do remember it, right? Of course, I thought of you, my Cherie, but it would have been rude of me to bring scraps. You deserve so much better. The number of beautiful people who still enjoy life is encouraging. Such stylish clothes and handsome couples danced and laughed like old times. You know?" Her words shocked me. Anger followed the shock.

"*You* know what, Genny, I don't know. You dare to enter my bed reeking with the scent of another man. I smell sex all over you. It repulses me. How dare you talk about the 'beautiful people last night.' You know who is beautiful? The French, American and British soldiers who lay forgotten on our battlefields. Get away from me? I find you disgusting and trashy, now leave at once!"

It did occur to me I ordered my hostess to leave her own little guest house, but at that point, I was thinking about locating a place of my own.

She laughed which annoyed me. *Does she laugh at me?* "Well, Victor, you may continue to act like a child. You must *wake up!* Life is not rosy as we once pretended. I merely want you to know; sometimes, you are not as smart as you believe. Okay, I am going to bed. Get some sleep."

Without another word, she stumbled from my bed. My world now felt rocked, confused. The irony of life glared sadly at me. Our roles reversed without any action from us. Immediately, I experienced the pain of the General as we caroused right under *his* nose. I now realized the depth of agony *he* suffered. How had he maintained his pleasant demeanor around me? A part of him must have hated me!

I realize this was horrible to say, but I kept thinking the same thing. *I wish she would simply go away. Her actions are impossible for me to bear.*

Sadly, I recalled the dress which she wore last night was new. Never would she call attention to herself by buying a dress like that so who purchased it? Did her "date" bring her lovely frocks as part of his arrangement to sleep with the most breathtaking woman in Paris? Suddenly, the shocking revelation of all hit me between the eyes.

Once again, denial had prevented me from earlier accepting the fact. Her officer was not a Frenchman. No, my VieVie La Fontaine had sunk to the lowest depth of depravity. She now galavanted around with a German soldier? Unable to control the bile from ripping through my system, I ran to the toilet. I heaved uncontrollably. Finally, I faced reality and didn't wrap myself in denial. Was this a German soldier who tore at the flesh of VieVie and admired her "*Frenchness?*" I hated them, and I felt fear for her. Last night, she had freely brought one of these monsters to our door. How long before this man returned during the light of day? Well, I knew the appeal of the lovely VieVie/Genny La Fontaine. The control which she easily stole from men was difficult to prevent. She played the game of sex and love skillfully. It would be impossible for a man to resume his normal life once he tasted of her allure and charm. Quickly, he would lose patience for his wife and children. Unknowingly, the German had bit into the essence of self-abandonment and turned his very life over to this, VieVie/Genny La Fontaine.

As the light changed from a cloudy, hazy day to the darkness of evening, I awakened with a start. *Have I slept all day?* Anytime I ever chastised my love, I quickly regretted it and feared she might never forgive me for unkind words. The hot shower felt divine as though I could remove the sins of my love. The smell, I once treasured, was now different as another man's scent mixed with her sweetness. Darkness penetrated the room as well as my soul.

Blackness surrounded the house on this depressing, dark evening in November. I shivered as I approached the main house. How stupid to have forgotten my coat! I deserve pain. *How could I level such anger at poor VieVie? She has deteriorated. Beyond a doubt, my love is crazy.*

It surprised me as I entered to find her dressed in a bathrobe with a towel around her head. Never had I seen her anything but perfection in every way at each time of day or evening. "Don't worry, I forgive you, Victor. Here, I have washed, even scrubbing away, the scent of my date. How do I smell now? Better? No sex smells, smell me." How can anyone be so direct?

"Only a while ago, I thought I heard you as you came inside, so I ran to hug you, but instead I noticed this box on our doorstep. It contains a meal for one, but it is very generous. Look, Victor, we have a lovely Beef Bourguignon for our dinner. Doesn't it smell divine? Wasn't such an action thoughtful of my date to think of me?" Innocently, she smiled as I shivered.

There was no use trying to alert her to the meaning of this "kindness." What it meant was the fact I knew and feared. Her "date" was thinking of her. It would be impossible for him to stay away now. Regularly, he would think of reasons to show at her home. Without warning, he could arrive at our door any time. *When will he discover me or the little house in the back? Will he think of me as suspicious? Will the interrogations soon begin? Have we sealed our fate? We deserve severe punishment!*

Nothing was important to me at that moment, but she does not harbor resentment toward me. Now, I understood her mindset; I could not feel bitterness toward her. To do so would destroy us. So, again, I shoved resentment, fear and betrayal down into my soul with the waiting feelings of shame for my treatment of my parents *and* the General. A large, dark hole in my mind filled with negative thoughts and severe pain. I should have talked to her and expressed myself, but I feared the loss of her love. Denial had become a way of life for most of us. We dealt with such harshness each day we did not voluntarily invite more pain through wordy discussions of our feelings. Life was too painful, too raw. It was easier to live in the constant state of denial, but at least there was some hope now because of the French Resistance and the brave allies who fought for our freedom. A new day would arrive. I could feel it. *Don't give up, not yet!*

Genny spent the day reading as she appeared to avoid my presence. I longed to hold her in a tight embrace and make her feel safe and truly loved, not used, but she would not allow such actions from me. My heart broke for her and the danger we now faced.

CHAPTER SIXTEEN

THE "DATES" CONTINUE

Two days later, the same scenario occurred. Early on a Monday morning, I entered the kitchen to find Genny sitting in her window seat. As she tried holding her head back to balance the cucumber slices, I smiled. "What, another date so soon? I guess he couldn't resist your charms."

The cucumber slices fell from her eyes as she laughed happily. "You are wrong, Victor. It is not the same 'date' as earlier. Tonight brings a new one; he is highly decorated and famous, much more than the last one. How joyful to eat delicious food once again and dance in the arms of a sexy officer!" I snorted as I attempted to keep my temper under control. Longing to explain as most of us starved, we were happy Madame La Fontaine enjoyed her charmed life.

"Victor, I have decided to change my name back to VieVie La Fontaine instead of Genny. VieVie sounds much gayer and freer. Don't you think? Suddenly, I feel young and elated with life again." This conversation appeared doomed, not in a peaceful direction for us. Already, I sensed an upbeat quality to Genny's demeanor. My depression had raged for days.

So, you are back to being VieVie, whatever pleases you, my love. Have you gained a little weight? Perhaps, the other German provides you with food which you have not shared? Maybe, VieVie, you have stuffed yourself with truffles and delicious chocolates inside the privacy of your room while I starve? All of this made me uncomfortable. I suspected such despicable qualities in someone who once hung the moon and stars at least in my mind.

"Victor, when will you begin *your* duties in the Resistance Movement? It is inspiring when you start to do something *important* with your life." Her sweet smile annoyed me beyond words. What exactly was she doing to "free Paris?"

"Well, VieVie, you know this is not discussable between us. Would you mind if I ask you what it is like to allow a German officer to grunt and groan as he ravages your body? Does he smell differently than a Frenchman? How can you do this for a good meal and new clothes?"

"*You* are a German; your father was as well. Don't classify yourself as a *Frenchman*. You will never be such, Victor. Your blood defiles you as you attempt to claim the French heritage. Never, will you be French! Did I complain at the scent of *you* or your father by the way! Nor did I mind when you groped and grunted with me!" The gaze from her eyes appeared angry and most hostile. VieVie's words surprised me since Mrs. La Fontaine was usually gentle. Our relationship had changed. Regularly, we began to parade around each other as though there was no alteration in our consistency, but we both knew our feelings for each other were not so rosy as in the past.

We must squelch this anger. The imperativeness of our closeness must survive if we were to continue together. More and more, I feared the resentment which I harbored for the woman whom I once adored. Often, I dreamed of turning her over to the French Resistance so they could humiliate her. *Can they make her stop these sinful actions? Does she even think of her husband?*

VieVie grabbed her extra cucumber slices and pranced from the room as my stomach growled loudly, I lowered my head. Life was becoming more and more unbearable as I waited for my demise. It was only a matter of time. The larder was empty as were my feelings for life. I envied the General and the fact he never had to witness all of this. If only he had survived. Maybe, his wife may not have completely lost her mind.

Perhaps, we can still feel a spark of joy for living again? Who knew the answer? How could a solution be found since we no longer trusted anyone? At any moment, a friend may be discovered to be a member of the Resistance who would grab VieVie as an example while another may be a collaborator and turn us over to the German authorities. It became more than any of us could bear.

Food no longer meant much to me. The weight was alarmingly dropping from my frame. I considered starving myself to end all of the drama. Death was a pleasant option. As I moved to VieVie's empty chair in the sun, there was a gentle knock on the door. Opening the massive structure, I smiled at a lovely young girl with a French, blue wool beret. Her smile surprised me.

Do the people in France still do this? Did people continue to laugh? More and more, conditions changed as the Vichy regime made us all angry. The news became increasingly offensive as there appeared no end to it.

Young people still smile?

"Oui?" *Can she read my mind?*

With one word, she quickly looked around; she handed me a bundle of leaflets. To my amazement, she turned and was gone. What was I supposed to do with all of these documents?

Where shall I pander my wares? Shaken, I received no education on the value of what I held in my hands; I walked back to the sunny spot feeling darker than earlier.

As I sat in my seat reading my little tract, I looked up to see a German officer smiling at me from the window in the door. Immediately, I began to shake and sweat dramatically. If there was ever a guilty imposter, it was I. Carefully; I stood so as not to drop my literature which would mean certain arrest for me. Meandering to the door, I attempted to appear unhurried and uninterested in this unknown character who waited with a smile. When I reached the door, I quickly ran toward the green cabinet and threw my leaflets inside it.

"Good morning, sir, it is a lovely morning." I spoke with my heaviest, fake French accent as I smiled with what I hoped appeared to be ease.

"Ah, you are the nephew of the lovely woman, it is popular to meet you." This German's English was not proficient, but I guessed VieVie had told him I spoke mainly English. My story was I spent a great deal of time in America. VieVie and I had tried to prepare for any possible situation. The German pushed me aside and looked around the house. Immediately, his eyes went to the green armoire. I began to perspire once again.

Apparently, he was her "date" for tonight. I understood the urgency of his position. Thoughts of how she dominated my earlier life shook me as I looked with pity into his blue eyes. "Um, I have a party tonight with VluVlu." He smiled.

I thought about correcting him but was aware how quickly these barbarians could turn. Instead, I smiled brightly at him. "Yes, Aunt *VieVie* has talked of you all morning. She is most excited to be with *you*. You are a lucky man." He nodded as he continued to walk around our house. Suddenly, his hands jerked something from his heavy coat. I fell backward in haste as I waited to feel the pistol shoved into my chest. Instead, he produced a bright red box. Again, he brightly smiled as he pushed it, not a gun, into my stomach.

"Please tell her these chaplets are for her. Also, tell her I long to carouse her greatly in my arms of sluve later this evening. My heart plops inside of my drawer just at the mention of her." He patted me firmly on the back, looked around the room once more as his eyes stared again at the green chest. He strutted toward it; he turned to glare at me. Curiously, he rubbed the surface of my favorite piece and opened the top door. His eyes seemed to take inventory of each item.

My deposit earlier was in the lower section which he did not seem to notice until he kneeled down and rubbed the wood on the very door which I had previously opened. Then he stood, laughed merrily, and walked past me. He turned to stare into my eyes once again. The door slammed as I collapsed onto the floor. For the longest time, I remained huddled on the cold floor. Life was impossible.

CHAPTER SEVENTEEN

MY MISTAKE

Immediately, VieVie ran into the room. "*Mon Cherie*, are you okay? I listened from the bedroom. What a close call that was. I should have prepared you that he may visit as my other date may show at any time. Don't forget; these monsters are our captors. They can do anything they wish."

As I sat up with embarrassment, I shunned her hand from my arm. "Here, VluVlu are your chaplets. Your next one longs to carouse you greatly in his arms of sluve. By the way, it was popular to meet him."

"Victor, did you hit your head? You are making no sense right now."

"Here's my point! How can you endure these idiots groping you? They can't even communicate properly. I hate them." Suddenly, I felt her small arms enfold me into the indescribable scent of vanilla. Long ago feelings overtook me. I reached for those ripe, full, pink lips. Their taste, I remembered well.

"Cherie, we must not. Instead, we need to make plans about every possible incident which may occur in the future. I had to extend an invitation to my dates; they would show anyway if they desired to come here. Not to invite them would have caused suspicion. I am not as undependable as you seem to think lately. You must trust me." She was correct. I had tried to minimize her, so I didn't appear inadequate in this situation, whatever it was. The woman whom I once loved looked at me with pity as I longed to hold her and feel her comfort me. The rest of the day, instead of her primping for the "great date," she worked with me about possible scenarios which might occur. If this happens, we must do this. If that happens, we must do that. Over and over we practiced our responses. When we completed our drill, I felt much relieved.

"Oh, no, I don't have long to prepare for my date. What will I do? I must look gorgeous. It is imperative I claim the affections of a certain officer. These others are merely fish in the pond. I must maintain my position."

What is she saying? How can I expect her to be rational? She is insane. With those words, she ran upstairs. Well, at least our refrigerator now stayed somewhat stocked with delicious little nibbles since VieVie's many dates. I thought jokingly about the "position" which she would soon assume. It sounds mean, but the humor was necessary. At least, I was finally able to laugh a little.

I hope your meal tonight is worth the shame and humiliation of having this brute grope you. Although I don't know, perhaps I will sleep with the pigs for a nice steak dinner. I laughed at the thought as I heated one of the small containers from Maxim's, one of the best restaurants in 1941 Paris. A slight knock at the door interrupted glorious thoughts of happy days at my place of enchantment. The "date" was early. Trepidation filled my heart as I moved slowly toward the door. Never would I adjust to this madness. My leaflets still rested thrown inside the green cabinet where I had deposited them earlier.

With undecidedness, I slowly opened the door. Smiling at me were large baby-blue eyes from under the edge of a navy blue, wool, French beret. It was my messenger from the Resistance. It surprised me she ventured out into the bright light of day. "Um, shouldn't you make your appearance at night? Isn't this dangerous for you and me?"

Roughly, she pushed me aside and entered the house. Without invitation, she helped herself to half of my meager dinner. Was she a German in disguise? Her greed sure mimicked one. "Ummm, where did you get this? This scrumptious fare is from Maxim's which is one of my favorite places in the city. Well, once upon a time, this was true. It is delicious!"

I almost cried as I watched her devour my little supply of food. Already, I was starving. Envy swept over me. Tonight, Mrs. La Fontaine would dine on the best of Paris. She would be allowed to eat all she desired. Heck, I *would* sleep with the Germans if they would feed me like this. Without thinking, I shoved these ridiculous thoughts into the depth of my heart as I studied the pretty, young, French girl. "So, you have eaten at Maxim's? I wouldn't have guessed it."

"Your words are very bigoted. You should learn things have changed for us all. You are no longer allowed to make such decisions based on another's looks or dress? Besides, what's wrong with me? Am I not worthy to enjoy such exquisite morsels?"

"Touché, I apologize for being such a pig. You are beautiful. Are you my supervisor?" Laughing merrily, she removed the wool beret from her dark locks which spilled quickly from confinement as they revealed the healthy, shiny hair of a little girl. Her pale blue eyes shined at me merrily. Suddenly, the young woman removed her heavy, dark blue jacket as she threw it onto the floor. She appeared robust with large breasts which pulled my eyes from her face. For the first time in months, I felt alive. Lust overcame me as we embraced.

All of this must sound like depravity but why not? Our life could end at any moment. We were young people led by leaders who should have learned their lessons. Instead, we were being forced to fight another battle. One which we did not desire but hated; watching our city occupied by heathens was extremely difficult. Witnessing our French women bend to the Germans created madness. Now, I believed, as did many, it would have been easier to die in these very streets than merely give them away. We all suffered terribly but could not know of the fate which awaited thousands. These hurt much worse than we. What they endured was a crime against nature we could never forget or deny.

Unlike my earlier gentle actions with VieVie, I ripped the clothes off this beauty. My movements with her were not tender or protective. I felt lust like an animal. She stood before me naked. Amélie was the exact opposite of VieVie. Her figure was full and voluptuous. The groaning which I heard was from me as I enjoyed the delights of her youth. We made love hard and quick. Our guttural sounds were those of animals. It was over in minutes, but we both were briefly relieved from the pressures of our daily struggles. Afterward, we lay on the sofa huddled together to stay warm under a heavy quilt. There was a firm knock on the door. As I looked out the window, a German officer peered at us with interest. What had I done?

CHAPTER EIGHTEEN
VIEVIE'S DATE

Shocked too drastically even to talk, I casually walked to the door in my underwear as though a friend waited for my greeting. The German officer entered. He smiled at me with curiosity as he continued to walk forward into our house. His arrogant ways made me spew with anger. He walked as though he owned the house. *Well, he can if he desires, but I still hate him.*

"What is this? *Geschlechtsverkehr?* Well, my, my, VieVie's nephew is it? Is this your girlfriend? What is your name, *Fräulein?*" What had I done now? I dreaded to even look at Amélie. Due to my eagerness to spend time with this beauty, I may have signed our death warrants. Without missing a beat, Amélie stood completely naked and walked toward the officer.

Is she insane? He could take her right here. She must know her actions are insanity. Is anyone left in control of their mental faculties? "Ah, yes, VieVie's date; so nice to meet you, *Oberbereichsleiter.*"

The officer smiled intently at the naked beauty who stood without any hint of shame before us. At that moment, VieVie entered the room. Somehow, despite the change in our roles, VieVie managed to take my breath away. Although she stood beside a voluptuous, much younger specimen, all eyes looked at her. Wearing an emerald green dress with sparkling emeralds on her ears and around her neck, I could feel the German drooling. No longer did Amélie receive his stares. He fell all over himself as he grabbed VieVie and kissed her for a long time and a little too firmly. *He is a swine.*

"We should go. I have reservations. We are to join General Schneider; I must not keep him waiting even for one as beautiful as you. Perhaps, you may want to instruct your nephew to entertain his girlies more privately?"

He wickedly laughed as he looked intently at me and lustfully at the French beauty. His earlier smiles suddenly evaporated into a stern and almost evil look. VieVie seemed ill at ease as she followed him to the door. As she turned to say, "Good night," I saw pain deep in her eyes; how well I knew that pain.

The resentment she felt toward this younger woman, I had experienced with each man whom she brought home. The same feelings, I felt when I thought of anyone else loving her. No longer did her "dates" cause me the degree of humiliation which I suffered earlier, but I continued to feel the sting as she pranced away with her German puppet. "Yes, Victor, you need to show some respect to your aunt. I tire of your escapades with these young women. Why not show some constraint?"

"Yes, of course, Aunt VieVie, as you do?" She gasped. Her German friend did not hear my words. It was foolish of me to play games like this, but I was a young man full of anger and resentment. My degree of self-control rapidly dissipated in such trying conditions. VieVie closed the door.

"Come on Amélie. Are you crazy prancing around in front of a German like that? They are violent thugs who now occupy us. He could do anything he wanted to you. Were you smart?"

" I realized how smart VieVie is and the fact, she would never keep him waiting. By acting as though I was an innocent, foolish, young woman *that* German would never even think of the matter again except maybe to lust a little. Don't worry, 'Aunt VieVie' will remove any images of *me* from his mind. VieVie La Fontaine has quite a reputation. She is a *un mangeur d'hommes* if you don't mind me saying."

"What does that mean, *un mangeur d'hommes?*" Amélie smiled wickedly.

" A man-eater, you do know what I mean?"

"Yes, I believe I am standing next to one."

How does she know so much about VieVie? I should have asked her but did not.

As we talked and laughed together, I realized how much I needed this intelligent woman who was a little younger than me. The earlier games with VieVie depressed and tired me as did life itself. When I held this young, thoughtful girl, I felt alive and in my element. Later, we moved to my little house in an attempt to stay warm. She loved my house as she told me she lived with different people and walked around steadily. Amélie did not have a home.

"Why can't you stay here with me? We are a good team. Will you consider it?"

"It would mean the world to me knowing where I will end up each evening or a shower waits for me although there is no longer anything such as a 'warm shower.'" Sadly, she smiled at me.

"Shouldn't you ask Aunt VieVie before extending such an invitation?" By the look in her eyes, I knew, she was aware of my relationship with my "Aunt VieVie."

"How do you know all of this? Your knowledge is a little frightening to me." Without a word, she climbed into my bed of fluffy butter-colored silk and smiled.

"Come on, Victor, ugh, Mark Lichter, we are the French Resistance Fighters. We are the people, who, with the help of our allies, will free Paris and all of France from these monsters of occupation. It is vital we work silently, swiftly and courageously to avoid their suspicions. The Germans are aware of us and how rapidly we multiply. Did they believe we would turn our country over without a fight? They have misjudged us. Every job is important in our movement. Now, come on, and I will show you how to disperse your weapon."

Her words confuse me. What weapon? "Victor, you must think! You have to be quicker. Your *leaflets*! You haven't begun to hand them out. Don't think we haven't been watching you! We count on our people to think without being led as children. Now, show me where you have stored them. We must get to work!"

"Do you mean now? Tonight? It is freezing." Amélie was already prancing across the yard covered in a heavy blanket. I followed her into the main house.

When she turned toward me, she hit me with a great deal of force shoving me into the wall. "Your words infuriate me! How do you think our soldiers and those of our allies would feel to hear your weak words? Do you not realize they are *freezing* huddled in those woods around France fighting for *our* day of liberation! What if they said, 'it is too cold tonight to fight?'"

Angrily, she looked around the room as though trying to discover the pamphlets. "Victor, you are *now* a soldier. You fight for the French Resistance. Your comfort and safety are about as important as mine and VieVie's. We don't matter individually. Together, we can set our country free! If some of us die, such is the consequence of our actions. Where are they?"

When I show her how casually I have thrown them into the little green cabinet, she will become even more furious with me. "Don't you want to go upstairs and tidy up? You may want to wash up?"

"No! Stop stalling. We must get to work. Now is the time to blend into the approaching darkness. Show me the documents!" Hesitantly, I approached the cupboard and opened the bottom door. Amélie gasped when she saw the documents thrown casually inside. Her eyes traveled from their location to the front door. She madly shook her head at me.

"Now, I must ask *you* if you are insane? Did you never consider at least two different Germans have stood inside this house? Either of them could have opened this door. Your execution, as well as your 'aunt,' would have occurred at great speed. Even worse than you are the hundreds of fighters who may have been compromised due to your silliness. Could we have made a mistake asking you to join us?" Amélie grabbed the leaflets and ran out the door.

CHAPTER NINETEEN
A NEW LOVE

Outside, the coldness hit me square in the face. Yes, I had grabbed my coat but in my haste had forgotten gloves and a hat. Paris no longer glowed like a jewel wrapped in the River Seine. She appeared lonely and dark. Her streets seemed to be empty and scary due to the curfews imposed upon us. I slowed my pace as I peered down long corridors of darkness. No longer did I harbor the fear of being arrested. If I suffered from the long arm of tyranny, so be it.

Anything was far better than hiding in the safety of VieVie's home. The more I walked in the black, frosty air, the more courageous I felt. Soon, I was able to see my surroundings as my eyes adjusted to the inky blackness. Silent figures weaved among the streets. Quickly, they darted in the shadows. Were they the Resistance? I eventually tired as it became apparent my new friend had evaporated into the bleak surroundings. Apparently, I chased a phantom. Reluctantly, I began my retreat back home. I hated returning to what had now become my prison. Merely being outdoors and feeling the current of danger electrified me, emboldened me.

Much too quickly, I arrived home. When I opened the door, a sense overcame me. *I am not alone!* That old terror rose up briefly, but I recalled the words of one younger and much wiser.

In the future, I must refuse to continue living in fear. Boldly, I entered my space as I prepared for a group of Nazis to arrest me. Instead, I saw a small lump in my bed.

"VieVie is it you? Your date did not go so well? He is swine!"

"No, Victor, it is I, Amélie. So sorry to disappoint you. Many nights have passed since I was able to sleep an entire night uninterrupted. May I stay here long enough for a small amount of rest? I will be on my way soon."

"No!" The lump raised slowly. Amélie's dark hair spilled into those lovely eyes as she looked curiously at me.

"No, I don't want you ever to leave me. Stay here until the madness ends. Together, we will fight the Germans as we take back our streets one lane at a time. With you by my side, I am fearless. Without you, I slink in distress. Here, you have a warm bed and a cold shower. I'm sure my aunt can find some clothes for you in her abundant wardrobe. Please, don't leave until this war ends." We laughed at my promise of a "cold shower."

"My dearest one, I predict before the war ends one of the three of us will meet certain death. I refer to myself, you and VieVie. You can be sure we will not all make it out of this alive. Yes, I will fight by your side for as long as we have the strength to fight." Suddenly, she fell back into a deep sleep. Her body was freezing. She seemed to convulse with the cold.

How long has she been living in the streets? How many cold nights has she shivered and tried to find warmth? What things has she done in the alleyways to stay alive? I held her firmly as I attempted to increase her body temperature. *How many of us fight silently for the liberation of Paris and France?*

"Vive la France!" Quietly I spoke those words as I looked at my new friend, my heart burned with admiration and respect. *I will also achieve those very titles in my new role of Resistance Fighter. It is imperative that I restore my sense of self-worth.*

CHAPTER TWENTY

CHRISTMAS OF 1941

Amélie taught me much about resistance techniques which did not always mean fighting the Vichy and Germans but messing up their plans. We began to rescue individuals threatened by persecution, mostly Jewish families like the one I saw much earlier in the street. Charitable groups attended Jews housed in camps. These eventually turned into lines of escape for the downtrodden, especially the poor, dear children. Never would I forget the little girl whom I sent to death without even a word of encouragement to her. Such was my cowardice; now, forced to live with her memory forever! Our actions became desperate when the powers of France and Germany started to gather Jews for deportation to concentration camps. They began with the foreigners quickly changing to the French.

Christmas of 1941 was nothing special to the average Frenchman. I suppose that to the Christians, it remained special for their reasons, but to most of us, it was another mundane day. Conditions stayed dire as people were rounded up in the streets for opposing the Germans. Communists fought beside our Resistance Fighters. To us, we didn't care about the political ideology of our fellow Resistance Members. What mattered was the pledge to fight our occupiers "till the death."

A new year approached as the brutally cold weather continued. Apparently, there would be no breaks for us. By 11 November 1942, German forces occupied the whole of France. Our entire country experienced an invasion by Northern attitudes aligned with Southern ones. German troops came together as their momentum grew. The most important development for our Resistance Fighters was the union of the British with us which proved instrumental in assisting the British officials to plan for their paratrooper's landings into France.

Acts of resistance in Paris continued to increase in danger. In the spring of 1942, five students of the *Lycée Buffon* protested the arrest of one of their teachers. This group composed of about one hundred students who chanted the teacher's name as they merely threw leaflets into the air. That was all! How dangerous were they? These demonstrators easily escaped. Still, the police arrested the five student leaders. Later, they were tried and executed. Such ridiculous overreactions caused all of us to live in fear. What if we looked at a German official in a way which he saw as offensive. Would we be executed? These Germans could get away with anything. It appeared laws did not apply to them. Of course, they didn't. *They are our occupiers.*

As the war continued into the spring of 1942, the Resistance appeared mainly divided into two groups, the followers of General de Gaulle in London, and the Communists. At last, thanks to pressure from the British weapon suppliers, and the bravery of one resistance leader, Jean Moulin, the *National Council of the Resistance* finally was established. Guided by his leadership, the different factions began to coordinate their actions. This combination of various factions was what had been lacking to catapult resistance actions to increased success!

What we all tried hard to prevent started on 23 May 1942, when the head of the Anti-Jewish section of the Gestapo, Adolf Eichmann, secretly ordered the deportation of French Jews to the concentration camp of *Auschwitz.* Conditions for the Jews continued to worsen as, on 29 May 1942, all Jews in the Occupied Zone over the age of six were required to wear the yellow Star of David Badge. How could they target children? We diverted our eyes when we saw these poor souls on the street. Most of us wanted desperately to help them. We realized to do so meant our death as well. In July, our officials banned Jews from all main roads, movie theaters, libraries, parks, gardens, restaurants, cafés and other public places. Eventually, they were required to ride on the last car of metro trains. The situation continued to worsen when on 16–17 July 1942, the Germans ordered twelve thousand three hundred fifty-two Jews (four thousand one hundred-fifteen children, five thousand one hundred-nineteen women, and three thousand one-hundred eighteen men) to be rounded up by the French police.

Eventually, the unmarried persons and couples without children were taken to *Drancy* about twenty kilometers north of Paris. Without providing food or water during the heat of summer, these innocents were herded to internment camps before eventually taken to the

Auschwitz extermination camp. The road to death for these tortured souls had begun!

During the summer of 1942, deportations to the extermination camps increased. Networks of Jews and Christians began to work together. Jews received assistance to the borders of Spain or Switzerland where they could make a safe break. Our feeling was we couldn't do enough.

Although there were tidbits of good news, the more reports we received, the worse things appeared for us. We felt helpless but continued trying to assist those targeted groups. Parisians began to feel as if they were starving to death which forced us to hunt for food anywhere we could find it. Rationing continued not only for food but clothing. Leather was reserved exclusively for the German army boots. Leather shoes became a luxury of the past as we now wore shoes made of rubber or canvas (raffia) with wooden soles. The products which we purchased often were not what we received. Many substitutions were unknowingly made without notice. We had no idea what we were buying.

We tired of being cold each winter as the shortage of coal only worsened. The authority over the coal mines of Northern France, the Germans, gave our supplies to *their* military headquarters in Brussels, of course. What little fuel Paris did receive was scheduled for the factories, not individuals, because of this, the black markets flourished in Paris. The bars of the Champs-Élysées and other parts of Paris drew those with money to these meeting places between the middle-men and clients. This black market was the only way for Parisians to buy cigarettes, meat, coffee, wine and other "luxury" products.

During this time, Amélie and I learned one of our heroes, Michelle, succumbed to pneumonia. Together, we hugged and cried at our loss. Our brave friend would have hated to die in such an ordinary manner. If we had to die, as we fought, all of us prayed to die at the hands of tyranny. It was better to die a martyr than a regular citizen. It became important to remember each of our people who died regardless of the way. They gave their lives for our cause. That was vital to our mission.

While most Parisians hungered and froze, not the beautiful women of Paris, who were willing to escort the Germans out to the best restaurants and theaters. Paris restaurants were open but forced to deal with strict regulations and shortages. They only served meat on certain days, and specific products: such as cream, coffee and fresh produce were scarce. Just the same, the better restaurants found ways to serve their regular clients and now the haughty Germans with their French "dates." For five hundred francs a good pork chop, hidden under cabbage and served without the necessary tickets, could be purchased along with a liter of Beaujolais and real coffee. Often it was on the first floor at *rue Dauphine*. While there, you could listen to the banned BBC as you sat next to a Picasso painting.

Is the world insane? Apparently, it was! As one may suspect, there was much plunder by the German occupiers. *The Galerie Nationale du Jeu de Paume* filled with art stolen from Jewish families. The Germans laughed of their conquests which sickened us to see those brutes carrying the hard work of our citizens away from homes which loved fine art. Houses where culture and kindness once flourished. Vermeer's painting, *The Astronomer*, unfairly was removed from the Rothschild family by the Nazis and given to Adolf Hitler. All of us were sickened by the news. One of the most significant art thefts in history happened in Paris during the Occupation. Nazis looted the art of Jewish collectors on an unheard of level. Inside the Louvre, great masterpieces had already been evacuated by French citizens to the *châteaux of the Loire Valley* where they were safe. The German Army surprisingly was respectful of the *Hague Conventions of 1899 and 1907*. They refused to transfer the works inside French museums from our country. Nazi leaders were not this scrupulous. Often, we witnessed them carrying priceless treasures with no attempt of cover.

Confiscations continued at banks, warehouses and private residences while paintings, furniture, statues, clocks and jewelry accumulated at the *Jeu de Paume* filling the entire ground floor. German propaganda appeared all over our buildings. A swastika hung at the Paris Opera for a festival of German music in 1941. No longer did we shed a tear at such taunts; we wanted action! Tears dried as their replacement became seething anger.

VieVie appeared to glow with health as young Amélie's glow waned. The younger woman's hair dulled as her brilliant blue eyes no longer burned with excitement. Each time I saw VieVie, anger infiltrated my heart. Often, I considered choking her as she openly flaunted her

German admirers. It no longer mattered to me that quite possibly she was insane. *Must she flaunt it so dramatically?*

Amélie lived with me in the little cottage for over two months while VieVie paraded her German general around for show. Now, she walked beside him as his escort. Down the Parisian streets, they strolled arm in arm. At least no other men would ravage her. Many of our French women, apparently VieVie was one, began to think the Germans were destined to win the war. They believed I guessed; they were on the "winning side." Life for many collaborators was in some ways better than past times. These traitors remained warm at night. Women like my Amélie disliked them as French women who cavorted with Germans wore stockings and perfume provided by their amours. When other French women walked past *their* German officers, the collaborators would pull on the arm of their companion or kiss him on the lips to prevent flirtations. No wonder many of us harbored resentment toward these people who gave up patriotism for their country so quickly.

On a late summer day, Amélie and I slept late. Together, we tirelessly had worked the night before. Whenever the British made a drop of our little papers, we formed lines to transport them back to the Paris streets. There, we worked fervently, sometimes foolishly, as we passed them out. Looking into the wrong set of eyes may be the last time we looked at anyone. Without warning, VieVie pranced into the room. "Oh, darling, I have missed you."

Her scent was clean from a recent bath unlike the smell from Amélie and me. As she rubbed against me naughtily, I pushed her away. Amélie sat up in surprise. "VieVie?"

"Yes, I am but who are you?" It never appeared vital that I explain to my *new* love that my *old* love was not aware I had a new "roommate."

"What are you doing in Victor's bed, I mean, *my* bed?"

"I live here. Why are you rubbing against *my* boyfriend?" VieVie laughed mischievously.

"Well, Markie, all of this time, I felt a little guilty about the way I treated you. Here you are with this lovely, younger woman. My, my, I suppose I am now free of any feelings for you. Yes, it is okay your whore stays here in *my* bed. Now, you see, I have a *real* man. He takes care of *me* instead of my having to provide for him. I will allow you and your munchkin to remain but only because I promised General La Fontaine to stay with you. To me, you are both despicable. Not to be concerned, never will I rat you out, but if *my* German general discovers the truth of you two, be prepared to join the concentration camps where *your* people receive the death sentence. She is one of you. Isn't she?" *Her words hurt.*

When VieVie hit Amélie on the backside, I wanted to break her hand, but my sweet Amélie grabbed my arm. With a warning look from those eyes of blue, I realized my folly. VieVie had always been correct; she was now one of the most influential women in France. I genuinely believe in her mind; this exalted position would never end.

CHAPTER TWENTY-ONE

MORE MADNESS

At this time, Paris had become the primary destination for the rest and recreation of German soldiers. The invaders had a slogan, Jeder einmal in Paris ("everyone once in Paris"). As time progressed, each German soldier received one visit to Paris during his stint in the military. One month after the beginning of the Occupation, a bi-monthly magazine and guide for visiting German soldiers called *Der Deutsche Wegleiter für Paris* (The German Guide to Paris) was first published by the Paris *Kommandantur*. Many hotels and movie theaters were reserved exclusively for these "special" German soldiers. A German-language newspaper, the *Pariser Zeitung* (1941-1944), was also published for the occupying soldiers. The German officers enjoyed the most excellent restaurants in Paris as the exchange rate was fixed to favor them. Many houses of prostitution existed in Paris. They began to cater to German clients. More frequently, so they might eat, we watched our Frenchwomen patronize the German men. Part of me felt their pain, but a part of me wanted to punish them for such cowardly actions! I couldn't help but think. *Just you wait until the Resistance finds you!*

Life felt encouraging with my new mate. Amélie received great respect from the Resistance Fighters. In the streets, she knew her way around. It seemed she could smell the Germans. We may be walking down an alley when suddenly, she pushed me in a different direction, or she would stoop under a pile of boxes as a squad of invaders approached. Call it impossible to count the number of times she saved my life that year. Wisely, she taught me much.

Late spring, 1942, it was a glorious evening as France felt the warmth from the sun for the first time in months. All day, the sun smiled gently on our French people. We flocked to the streets. One could even see a smile or two. Amélie and I strolled fearlessly among the crowd.

"What do you say, let's stroll past Maxim's? Perhaps we can't afford to dine, but we can breathe the delicious smells. If we breathe deeply enough, I'll bet we can transport some of the food into our stomachs." Happily, we laughed as we briskly walked in that direction. How glorious walking together in the fresh evening air felt instead of hiding in dingy alleyways. With great joy, we continued along on our journey. Glancing to my left, I looked at the girl whom I madly loved. Our time together was happy while we did something vital for the freedom of our country. No longer did I look at my life with embarrassment as though I was a freeloader and imposter. Now, Amélie walked with me, I felt like a complete man.

"Oh, Victor, I can smell *that* smell. How many times have I scurried past the enchanting entrance to this mecca of delights! My boyfriend and I dined here frequently many years ago. That was before the madness began." *Are those tears on her cheek? Never has she shared anything about her personal life with me.*

Amélie suddenly quietened with her story as a faraway look glazed over her expression. I wanted desperately to hear the rest of her story but was afraid to interrupt her. To do so may cause her to clam up as was her nature. Almost as though speaking to herself, she continued.

"You would have liked him. Yes, the two of you would have been great friends. His name was Gabriel Martin. His stature was much like yours. Gab was very tall and skinny. We loved to run together in the streets of our beloved Paris. The Martins were wealthy. Maxim's rated as our favorite dining spot. Often, we joined his family here. They were a large and rowdy lot. Oh, I loved spending time with them."

Longingly, we stared at the entrance as we stood in front of the legendary Maxim's whose facade was posh and trendy. Tourists stopped to take a photo at the spot where most could not afford to dine. In these days of want, that was primarily the case. Together, we stood there in front of the place taking in the beauty of the wood and the red awning with golden letters which spelled *Maxim's*. Amélie leaned against the building. She appeared comfortable enough, so I stood beside her. We each put a foot on the building for support. She looked at me and smiled. It seemed she needed my approval to discuss this man from her past. I laughed and nodded at her. Then she began.

"Gabriel and I joined the Resistance early in 1941. His parents begged us to reconsider. After becoming engaged, I was considered part of the Martin clan. I loved it." My mind recessed to my little family consisting of myself, Hans and Abi. *There aren't many Lichter's who made it alive from past persecutions. Today, there are even fewer.* I shook away the fetters of sadness and concentrated on her story.

"I was the one who pushed Gab into joining the group. Already, I was involved and spent much time away from him. Maybe, he knew he would eventually lose me if he didn't join us. Anyway, we worked in the same way you and I do today. Mainly, we picked up brochures and distributed them as well as creating havoc for the Germans in any way possible. One day, we became careless. We discussed this town was *ours*, our place, not theirs. As we walked blatantly down the street with the leaflets in our hands, a group of Germans shouted for us to 'Halt!' Instead, we ran. Often, our captors were fat and unable to run. These were lean. They chased us. When we continued to avoid them, a shot rang in the light of a bright blue day. Gab dropped. I faltered, but they were now coming quickly. I saw the shooter aim at me. Out of nowhere, Michelle appeared and pushed me in front of her. Our run continued until we found safety. Yes, we saved *my* life but my beautiful Gabriel, I left him lying in the street. My solace is I'm pretty sure he was dead. He didn't suffer any further atrocity from them. That is my solace." No words passed.

What can I say? Instead, I kissed her hand. We stood in front of the famed dining spot between *Place de la Concorde* and the *Madeleine, on rue Royale.* Together, we spied the spot loved by many, located in the heart of Paris, not far from the Eiffel tower. Amélie turned toward the window of her beloved dining spot. Slowly, she breathed; I assumed she smelled the familiar smells which she loved. As she took my hand, a look of shock overcame her. Pointing inside she appeared pale; I pushed my face to the window. Several seconds passed before my eyes adjusted. It was so bright and gay inside. The interior was fancy, most impressive. Carefully, my eyes scanned the crowd of "the beautiful people," who weren't so beautiful to me. Mostly Germans, with our French women, laughed as they enjoyed the finest of France. The Art Nouveau decor welcomed them with a sense of culture. Pale pink tablecloths clothed small tables for two. The back of the room contained a long, red baguette. Laughter peppered outside for us peons to share the happiness inside the bright red and green interior where the people who believed they were "special" congregated. The effect of the designing of the interior was stunning.

As I continued to scan the room, my vision improved. My view ended at the table in the window front right before me. There sat VieVie La Fontaine dressed in a bright yellow dress. Her hair had grown since I last saw her. I realized I had not seen her in months. Lately, my work with the Resistance and Amélie claimed all of my time. Instantly, I became aware VieVie must now live with the General.

"Amélie, how long since we last saw VieVie? I haven't missed her since you came into my life." She sadly smiled as she explained VieVie's new German general had left his family in Berlin when the war began.

Did he expect to find a pretty, little Parisian to share the opulent space which he would receive? After only one week of time with her, he had invited VieVie to share his mansion, located in the *8th arrondissement,* close to the home General La Fontaine had shared with VieVie. I smiled. *Leave it to her to catch the biggest fish!*

My eyes watched as she fed the general a large piece of meat. The German seductively licked her fork. They laughed as their heads met gently. Then, the pig kissed her lips. VieVie returned his kiss in a hungry and depraved manner. My heart broke for her. *Doesn't she realize we, French, are beginning to gain a little in our conquest to liberate Paris? What will happen when our troops return?*

Already, neighbors, of the La Fontaine's, hated us. How many stood at the windows on the street by her new home watching the German officer come and go with her? Now, she openly lived with a German general? *Does she believe she will be allowed to continue her blessed life as before?*

What I felt were mixed feelings. I wanted to protect VieVie and ensure her well-being. Had I not promised General La Fontaine of such? Still, watching her so willingly kiss the lips of the enemy sickened me. Now, maybe Madame La Fontaine felt important, untouchable in her grand position, but what about when the French troops returned? *What will happen if the French Resistance get hold of her?* They hated this type of traitor behavior.

As I continued to stare inside, another German officer approached the table of Mrs. La Fontaine. I wondered if she ever thought of her husband? The German soldier was a lesser rank than her new love, but her general appeared pleased to see him. "Heil Hitler!" They saluted. I grimaced. VieVie laughed and clapped her small hands in delight.

Does she consider this one of her games? Don't the Germans know she is not well mentally? Plainly, this general must see signs of her mental instability. It was now apparent; she was not well. Of course, that German would not care. Mrs. La Fontaine kept him warm at night and entertained him each day. Why should he care what he was doing to an innocent woman? I called her *innocent* because she was insane.

Meanwhile, our resistance fighters continued their secret war. These brave warriors sent intelligence about German forces to the allies by a radio transmitter. They exhausted every way they could to help us win back our city as they published and distributed flyers and newspapers to counter both Vichy and German propaganda with the ideals and aims of the Resistance.

Finally, in November of 1942, the Zone became occupied by the Axis Forces leading to the disbandment of the German army. Only four Vichy officials received justice for the crimes committed against humanity although there had been massive deportations of Jews to the death camps for extermination. These individuals also were charged with crimes of inhumanity against the Resistance.

Each night, I thought of VieVie and her deadly actions. It was only a matter of time before she would be forced to face her blatant moves with these German men. Thoughts of what waited for her filled my heart with fear and sadness. There was nothing I could do to help her, so I watched her spiral into danger. *VieVie, how can I save you? I still profoundly love you. It seems I always will feel responsible for you.*

CHAPTER TWENTY-TWO
SOME GOOD NEWS, SOME BAD, 1943

Arrests of the Jews continued in 1943 and 1944. By the time of the Liberation, approximately forty-three thousand Jews from the Paris region alone, which equaled about half of the population from our community, were shipped to the concentration camps and death.

The Germans supported the creation of Vichy France. On 28 February 1943, a fascist paramilitary organization, the *Front Révolutionnaire National,* whose active police branch *Milice* formed. They would now assist the Germans against our resistance. They qualified as being a "terrorist" organization as they established headquarters in the former Communist Party building at *44 rue Le Peletier* and *at 61 rue de Monceau.* The *Front Révolutionnaire National* organized a substantial rally on 11 April 1943, at the *Vél d'Hiv.*

The news wasn't all bad. 13 April 1943, Jean Moulin, the most important figure of the French Resistance, parachuted into France. His noble actions provided tremendous encouragement to our people. In fact, a glimmer of hope continued to spread when in mid-June 1943, the constant talk of another Resistance fighter who loomed "larger than life" increased in circulation. This mammoth of a man apparently could sneak through German lines and do the impossible. With his emergence, hope also continued to grow.

Lately, all Amélie talked about was this "hero of the Resistance." I doubted if he existed but figured someone made him up to inspire us. If hope could shine from eyes such as hers, it didn't matter to me if it was a lie. "So anyway, the word is he led this group of paratroopers right under the German noses and into safety. What is happening is beyond belief! Many say the end of occupation is almost over. What say ye?"

"Um? Oh, I don't know. This hell may be the life we are forced to endure forever. I know I'm negative, but it is impossible for me to believe this may be over. There are as many who think the Germans are here to stay and their evil faces will occupy us forever. I like your scenario better." Amélie looked at me with disappointment. We all wanted to believe the war would soon end, but I refused to buy into these stories of a "Savior of the Resistance Movement." Such tales were a little convenient for our side.

"Anyway, so, what do you think will happen to people like VieVie if we finally end this thing?"

"Are you asking me what we should do with collaborators?" For a few moments, we argued about the term collaborator and if it applied to the French women who "dated" German soldiers. I believed they did no harm. It wasn't like they were passing on classified information. Most of those women were guilty only of being extremely beautiful and hungry. I wasn't entirely kidding when I jokingly said; I would sleep with the Germans. *Hunger and cold are becoming a little difficult to bear.*

"Look, Victor, any way you want to slice this, VieVie is a collaborator. How do you think our soldiers are going to feel about these women when they come home? Your former love was married to a famous French general. She must know all sorts of details and enticing facts. I can pretty well guarantee she will not receive pity because she was cold, hungry and tortured. We all are!" Her words frightened me for VieVie.

What will happen to these people who make things a little more comfortable for our occupiers? Although, I can't believe VieVie would pass on French information to the enemy. How bad would it be for them? Such thoughts were another new worry for me, what would happen exceeded my worst nightmares.

As the Germans stepped up their attacks on our Resistance, we, the Resistance fought even harder at outsmarting them, but there were other problems. The *Service du travail obligatoire* (English: Compulsory Work Service; STO) established the forced enlistment and deportation of hundreds of thousands of French workers to Nazi Germany. Once there, they worked as forced labor for the German war effort during World War II. The beginning of the STO created the program which required our people to work in German factories. The Germans reasoned this was fair as they returned older and sick French prisoners of war in Germany back to France. Such actions substantially increased the resentment of the French population against our captors.

Most Parisians, however, only expressed their anger and frustrations in private, while the police of Paris, under German control, every day received hundreds of anonymous denunciations by Parisians against other Parisians. Betrayals from friends were rampant.

The German powers suddenly demanded two-hundred-fifty-thousand workers from the STO of France. In April, one-hundred-twenty-thousand was the requirement. Their demands continued to increase as in May, they asked for one-hundred-thousand for June. Then, on 6 August, they became even more insane with their numbers. They requested five-hundred thousand on 6 August which didn't occur. Finally, the Germans ended STO when an agreement with the French government eradicated the madness. The workers received protection while our companies became entangled in the German economy.

During the summer of 1943, there was a surge to join the *Maquis/ French Resistance* and avoid forced labor. Unofficial figures mentioned two-hundred thousand people being taken away for forced labor with fifty-thousand escaping, many of whom joined our fight. More than thirty-thousand fled France into Spain or North Africa and joined the *FFA*. For those who did not want to fight or find a place in the Resistance, they remained hidden at home or on isolated farms with the help of accomplices. Many people were merely forgotten as the German bureaucracy became submerged in paperwork.

On 7 June 1943, René Hardy, an essential member of the Resistance in France, was arrested and tortured by Klaus Barbie and the Gestapo. They eventually obtained enough information also to arrest Jean Moulin, Pierre Brossolette and Charles Delestraint. Soon, after months of torture by the Nazis on a train, while being transported to Germany in 1943, our beloved hero, Jean Moulin was killed. All of us devoted patriots felt deep sorrow. In the streets, eyes were red and swollen. *Our loss is great.*

Brossolette was also tortured and eventually shipped with Delestraint to *Dachau* where they were killed near the end of the war. One day, there was talk of the end of the war, the next, our Resistance dwindled. Times were chaotic for all of us. Thinking with clarity did not exist.

In December 1943, Joseph Darnard, a fanatical anti-Communist, became chief of the secret police in Vichy. *The Milice* consisted of thirty-five members, many of them were fascists, who played an important role in investigating the French Resistance. Like the Gestapo, the *Miliciens* were willing to use torture to gain information.

Despite all of this, the rumors continued about a "Savior of the Resistance." This man who maneuvered right under the nose of German generals. He represented and fought not only for the Frenchman but any allied member who faced the giant arm of the Germans. All of these stories invariably were embellished if there was any truth to them. Hope was kept alive by the dream that there was an end in sight. I prayed this was the truth because, for many of us, it was hard to remain positive in the face of such unfairness. Would this hell ever end? My little French lover's appearance frightened me as she lost weight and seemed to be slipping away from me. *How can I help Amélie? Is she going to perish? One moment, life encourages me to move forward. The very next, I am pushed back to weeks earlier in this game of staying alive!*

CHAPTER TWENTY-THREE
CHRISTMAS 1943

"Well, another year has passed as we remain under the thumb of the Germans. How much longer can this continue?"

"Haven't you heard, Victor, my love? Our 'Hero of the Resistance' acted bravely once again right under the nose of the barbarians. Our reports state he aided the safety of twelve paratroopers and the crossing of over a hundred Jews into Switzerland. Don't give up yet." Amélie smiled sweetly. All I desired was to lavish her in warmth. I remembered the heavenly scent of vanilla which once surrounded VieVie whom we never saw any more. She continued to live with her German general in a mansion close to the Presidential palace. This home once belonged to a Jewish family, but the Nazis confiscated it when the family received death sentences to a concentration camp.

Now, the German and his beautiful whore, VieVie La Fontaine, entertained lavishly. The neighbors talked about the loud music which blared and beautiful cars which paraded in the circular drive all hours of the night. Reports stated there were drunken brawls as the Germans fought over each other's girlfriends. Was one of the fights over VieVie?

So much time had passed since I watched the spectacle she made in Maxims many months earlier. Her main house remained locked, so Amélie and I were unable to enter. I felt gratitude that my previous lover allowed us to continue living in her guest house but feared for the safety of one so fragile as she. Anger ignited all around Paris toward these French women who the Parisians labeled as "collaborators" for their actions with the Germans. Such blatant parties and strutting down the street as they enjoyed the most exquisite meals provided by their German lovers became more difficult for regular citizens to ignore. Watching such behavior, while the children of France barely had enough to survive, caused tempers to flare all around us.

Amélie and I seldom mentioned VieVie. To do so was painful for me as I sensed the anger which my new love harbored toward her. This anger, I well understood. Often in the evenings, we hid strategically located around the city as we observed actions of the Germans. These German officers and their French lovers now blatantly appeared to showcase their abundant stations while they occupied confiscated homes of Jewish families. As we froze, they opened the draperies of their lavish homes and allowed us to glimpse lives which we once enjoyed. Those halcyon days seemed like a distant dream.

Another summer passed without much change in our conditions. Winter was upon us again as we continued our attempts to remain warm. So much sickness assailed our people due to a lack of coats and proper cold weather gear. Still, our Resistance fought without concern for their well-being.

Having returned from a trek to the border of Switzerland with a group of Jewish young people, we were exhausted. All I could think of was going to bed and pulling Amélie close to me for warmth. We were terrified of pregnancy, but staying warm was vital.

"Please, Victor, let me go to Maxims and breathe the warm air as the door opens. If I may only smell the delights from the kitchen, this causes me such happiness." Apparently, she had brain damage. Her request would result in added time outdoors. My hands were blue already, and I could barely feel my fingers. Where did she get this incredible endurance? *Her genes must be better than mine.*

When I looked into her gentle blue eyes, I could not deny such an innocent request. I caved as we walked in silence toward her beloved restaurant. It occurred to me; she may be dreaming of another man, an earlier love, instead of her request to "smell the enchanting aromas." "Do you often think of Gab?"

She turned to me with fire in her eyes and a smile which she never offered me. The answer was clear even though she attempted to hide her feelings. *Gabriel owns her heart.* Her love for me was merely a way to continue forward with a sad and depressing life. Never could I make her happy as he had done. Even though together we fought now for the same cause, our fights were not as daring or grand as hers with the "great Gabriel."

When we arrived at Maxim's, a large party of German officers gathered in front. They appeared drunk already at this early hour. Some argument continued to heat as they postured around in the street. Words angrily assaulted the space.

"I'm asking you again, did you sleep with my girlfriend while I was away?"

"Why don't you ask *her*? Ask your girlfriend!"

Amélie touched my arm. "That is VieVie's general, is it not?" Carefully, I studied his face. It sounded like him, but I couldn't be sure. Then, the officer pushed a young woman away from the crowd. Alone the small figure stood in the street. She appeared to laugh at all of the drama. She was drunk.

Yes, it is VieVie. "You silly, bad boys, what is wrong? Why does it matter who sleeps with whom? Let's face it; we are not in *love*. We will all die. Every one of us will perish! Don't pretend to be normal. Let's merely have fun. Yes, we have orgies now and again. So what? We should all live life!"

In her drunken stupor, she turned toward the crowd as she held a drink into the air "What's wrong with *you* stupid people? Don't you see the Germans will win this war? Lay down your arms! Side with us and enjoy the good life again! Our time is short! *Heil Hitler!*"

Stumbling toward "her" general, she threw herself into his arms. As she rubbed against him, her hair of spun gold fell gently into her azure-blue eyes. He ripped her dress opened exposing her naked body for all to see. The crowd gasped. Some of the French women hid their eyes. Around me, the Frenchmen laughed angrily and sarcastically as the general began to kiss her roughly. Was this the way they spent their time? Did drunken orgies await them when they were not on assignment? We all looked at each other in shock. The crowd started to break apart as we quietly whispered disparaging comments into the air at the group of Germans.

"You whore, you'll pay France back for your transgressions. Who do you think you are? We know who you are Mrs. La Fontaine. You were married to a great patriot but shacked up with a young Jew under his nose. We know you and will never forgive you."

Almost five years had quickly passed since my earlier affair with VieVie. My appearance changed dramatically due to stress and dealing with the savagery of the times. VieVie had barely changed at all. Finally, she gained some weight which was most becoming. Her attire was of a woman with means. I looked at her with deep sadness because I realized France would be the winner of this war. The tide was changing as our Resistance, and the allies gained ground. There were no predictions on the date, but at some point, in the not too distant future, they would sign an armistice once again. When that happened, what waited for her? *God, please help the "collaborators." They will pay a substantial cost for the security they now enjoyed.*

"Enjoy your French whores, you German slime, your day is coming!"

"Who said that? Which of you frogs shouted such a nasty threat to us? Umm?" All of our group turned to walk away, but I looked once more at the woman whom I loved long ago. So much had happened since those days of our beginning in 1933. Barely could I remember her scent or the way she felt in my arms. My only thoughts were of Amélie and the love which we now enjoyed. Still, I knew the day would come and soon when VieVie would regret her shameful actions. On that day, no one would be able to save her from the hatred of her French brothers and sisters.

She is a turncoat of the worst possible kind. They would never forgive her. Again, I turned for one last look. At that moment, she pulled away from the general. She licked her luscious pink lips loudly and took another swig of her drink. Weaving, she walked to the edge of her party and stared into the street. Our eyes met. Recognition showed on her face. Her hand extended into the air as she pointed right at me. I should have run but could not. Frozen, I stood as I looked at her in horror. Amélie remained by my side. VieVie's eyes felt glued to my face. She opened her mouth as though she would speak but instead, smiled as she yelled.

"Vive la France!" Her shout was a high pitched yell. It sounded like an animal in pain. Tortured was the feeling I felt at that moment. Never would I forget the second in time when she had the power to destroy Amélie and me. Instead, she wanted me to understand. The pain which she shared, at that moment, was horrendous as her guttural yells filled the air. The sound was raw and animalistic. It was most evident; they destroyed her very soul.

VieVie has lost her soul. No one else could understand. Only Amélie and I got it. We waited. If this was our time to meet our God, so be it. Instead, VieVie held her empty glass into the air and hurled it at us. We turned and sauntered away. As we rounded the corner, I turned again to see the German general guide her inside the restaurant. Amélie's face covered in tears. She felt the pain of a crazed and tortured soul. Only I truly understood what she had tried to tell me. Later, the truth would present itself, and I would fully understand the pain in her bitter voice at that fateful moment. I recall the time well when her very look touched my soul. I seemed to understand what she tried to say with her eyes and the pain in her voice.

I realize I will never be the same. Happiness as I once knew won't grace my sad and demented life. You have no idea what I have sacrificed for my country. Our love is lost forever! Now, I understood! Her screams spoke to my soul! How could I have doubted her?

<h1 style="text-align:center">CHAPTER TWENTY-FOUR
Amélie's CHOICE</h1>

No words passed between us as we trudged home in the freezing night. All I desired was sleep and respite from the pain. My body was numb not just from the cold, but also from the horrible scene I had witnessed. We entered our little house together. Amélie went to the toilet as I stood by the window watching the platanes move gently in the wind. *Is there no end to this pain? What will become of VieVie? Am I the only one who understands her plight? She is very ill. Madame La Fontaine is insane.*

When I turned at a noise, which I figured was Amélie, a great form stood from the chair in the corner. My instincts told me the Germans had become suspicious from Vie Vie's earlier performance. I held my hands into the air expecting to be beaten and arrested. "Hello, Victor. It seems we share a love for the same woman. How are you?"

"Not so good at the moment, but you are wrong. I no longer feel love for Madame La Fontaine, only pity. Can't people see she is not well? Can she be held accountable for her actions?"

"Ah, the lovely Mrs. La Fontaine, but you see, I refer to the woman whom you *now* claim to love. Does the name *Amélie* ring a bell?" I staggered forward. The stranger's words hurt. He had diminished the love which I strongly possessed for Amélie. At that very moment, she stumbled into the room. She appeared pale. We were both exhausted from nights of trudging through the snow. We must have some sleep. No one could think clearly, not now.

"Who are you? What's going on? Victor, who is this?" I shrugged my arms as I looked at her with surprise.

"Amélie, my love, do you remain as such?"

"I don't know who you are. Why do you refer to me as 'your love?'"

"Darling, it is I. It is Gabriel." Amélie gasped as she fell onto the bed. Shaking her head, she stared from the man to me with confusion.

"No, this can't be happening. Gab died years ago in the street when he caught a German's bullet. I watched this. I hate to admit that I left him bleeding out in the street of Paris."

"Yes, you are correct. The Nazis did shoot me, and you *did* run, but two Resistance Fighters ran to me. Without regard for their safety, they carried me from the German brutes. These kind souls took care of me for months. After suffering from a massive infection and head trauma from my fall, I awakened with amnesia. No memory proved to be a good thing. It catapulted me into a fearless, almost robotic state. It is I, Gabriel Martin, or the 'Savior of the Resistance.' Only two days ago, my amnesic state lifted. Of course, I remembered the woman of my dreams. I had never forgotten you, Amélie, only your name and where to find you. Amélie, the war will end soon. I would like to leave before the finish. Believe me; I'm not a hero. When the end comes, my fighters will try to buoy me to hero status. All I desire is to live my life quietly with the woman whom I love more than any other in this world upon the mountains of Switzerland. We can come back to Maxims for a lovely dinner as in 'our' days. Do you still desire to be with me or do you share a more profound love with this, Victor? Whatever you decide, I will accept. Only, you must select now. When the allies arrive, and they are coming, we must be gone. Choose now, my love."

The light from a full moon shined onto the face of a man of extraordinarily good looks. The moving platanes outside the window moved the silver glow over his handsome countenance. His stature was tall and thin. Blonde hair with eyes of blue seemed to soak up the silvery light from the moon. Many cuts and scars only added to his appeal. Carefully, Amélie studied his eyes. Then, she turned to me. I knew as soon as our eyes met. Tears gently flowed down her cheeks. Pain projected from her onto me. I understood. Their dreams were strong. Ours were a rebound. Before she could speak, I kissed her gently on the lips. The salty tears caressed my lips. Softly, she touched my cheek.

"Victor, you know I loved you. It was real but my love for Gab....." Emotion grabbed her voice as Gabriel picked her up and wrapped her inside of his strong arms. Quickly, she kissed his cheek, then wiggled from his arms. Their passion was apparent, but I understood my darling did not want me to witness it. She grabbed her coat and looked at me once more. Never had she appeared more lovely than that moment in the shining light of a full moon. Her smile was happy. I couldn't cry.

"Be safe, my love. I will always love you, Amélie. Take care of her, Gab." Thrusting his large hand into the air, he motioned acceptance of my request. Silently, they turned and were gone. I fell into my bed of down and smiled. How ironic life appeared to me; our liberation was near, but I seemed to have lost everything. I could not know how massive my loss was about to become. *What is the point of going forward?*

CHAPTER TWENTY-FIVE

1944 LIBERATION AT LAST!

As the Normandy invasion approached in early 1944, the Communists and their allies ran the most aggressive resistance fighters in France. They were referenced as the *Francs-Tireurs et Partisans* (FTP). In February 1944, the FTP became part of a larger umbrella organization, the *Forces françaises de l'intérieur* (FFI). Following the Normandy invasion on 6 June 1944, (DDay), the FFI prepared to launch an uprising to liberate the city of Paris before the Allied Armies and General de Gaulle's arrival.

On 15 March 1944, the *Conseil National de la Resistance* published a charter demanding the implementation of a series of social and economic reforms after the liberation of France. These demands would equalize France and provide unknown benefits for her people. Most of us doubted this would happen, but it created deep excitement and increased hope for our future. We all longed to have faith again.

Later in the month, the German Army began a campaign of repression throughout France. Our aggressors launched several attacks against civilians living in towns and villages close to the French Resistance strikes. Their objective seemed to be demonstrating to our population the pain which we suffered was the result of the Marquis and our tolerance for it.

Yes, Paris realized the days of our captors approached their end. Our French Resistance needed to build up their attacks on our enemy. We weren't celebrating in the streets, no, not yet, but we were now able to accept a free Paris approached. There were few tales of the "savior of the Resistance," but I knew he took his love to a peaceful, unknown life in Switzerland. I envied them. My life appeared broken as our days of liberation approached. I should have been dancing in the street but could not find any joy. Instead, I experienced terrible nightmares as my dream of long ago would not give me respite from the tortuous visions.

Frequently, my loved ones, who walked sadly to that form in the future which I was still unable to see, were not only Hans and Abi but the General, VieVie, and others. Was the skinny man who followed behind them, me? They all ventured toward that large structure with downcast eyes. They refused to lift their eyes at my calls. I yelled their names, but they would not or could not raise their heads. Often, I saw the little girl whom the German guard pushed toward me years earlier. The very one whom I refused to even encourage out of my fear. Other familiar faces, which I had seen suffer abuse, also marched in the line of doom. Michelle now trudged slowly and sadly in this line of the tortured. These nightmares awakened me with a sense of panic. I sat up shouting and heavily sweating, unable to quiet the disturbance in my soul.

No joy remains for me! All appeared doomed. When the war ended, and it seemed that was only a matter of months, VieVie faced horrible retaliation from the citizens of Paris. I shook my head in dread for what must confront her. All I desired at this moment was sleep. The more I slept, the more I needed. Food no longer interested me. It was impossible to remember the last time I had eaten, but I continued to drink water. I was not ready to die, not yet.

Periodically, I would shake myself from the shackles of sleep to listen to the news. There were reports that the number of Resistance Fighters had increased to one-hundred thousand members. Our number had grown magnificently although the great "Savior of the Resistance" remained missing. I now knew that person was Gabriel and he lovingly harbored the beautiful Amélie within his strong arms each night. Those thoughts made me smile even if my heart broke.

Now, we knew our liberation was coming, but I felt no joy for myself. I did feel relief for the people in France and all of the Jews in Europe. On 5 June 1944, General Dwight Eisenhower asked the BBC to send out coded messages to the Resistance. They were asked to carry out acts of resistance during the D-day landings. Their actions would assist the Allied forces in establishing a beachhead on the Normandy coast. The bravery, those troops displayed, would never be forgotten. This resistance included attacks on the occupied garrisons in the towns of *Tulle* and *Gueret.* In revenge for the French attack on the German garrison one-hundred and twenty men were hanged in Tulle on 9 June. Later, another sixty-seven were murdered in *Argenton.*

Bravely, armed resistance groups were able to slow down the attempt by the *2nd SS Panzer Division* to get to the Normandy beaches. At that time, the Germans decided to carry out a revenge attack aimed at frightening the French people into submission. On 10 June, a group of soldiers led by Major Otto Dickmann, entered *Oradour-sur-Glane,* a village in the *Haute Vienne* region of France. He ordered the execution of more than six-hundred men, women and children, before setting fire to the town.

Despite these atrocities, the French Resistance continued to take up arms against the German army. After the war, General Dwight Eisenhower wrote the following: "Throughout France, the Resistance had been of inestimable value in the campaign. Without their great assistance, the liberation of France would have consumed a much longer time and meant greater losses to ourselves."

"Fight on brave Fighters! I should join you, but I don't have the heart." *I doubt if I even have one remaining.*

Often, I would rise from my bed and shout words of encouragement loudly into the empty air to my brothers and sisters of the Resistance. My thoughts remained hijacked by my fears for dear VieVie. What waited for her may be worse than death. I could only imagine the shame and degradation waiting from the angry hands of the French troops and patriots of France. She would never explain her actions. How well I knew the beauty. Before she revealed her actions, she would prefer death. The Resistance must be there to defend her.

I heard myself laughing heartily at my insane rambling of shouts for support of my beloved Resistance Fighters but felt nothing for myself. No joy, sadness, or relief did I experience. Nothing did I know except fear for VieVie and the terrible loss over Amélie's choice.

Parisians heard the sound of distant artillery fire in the capital on 8 June 1944. Trains filled with refugees, who departed *Gare d'Austerlitz,* with no announced destination. On 10 June, the French government fled Paris. Immediately, thousands of Parisians followed. All of these excess people resulted in a massive traffic jam as cars stalled and backed-up in our streets. In no time, the wealthier arrondissements of Paris sat nearly deserted.

Not knowing what else to do, I only watched once again the descent into madness and depravity in what once was a city of kindness and acceptance. Between 19 August to 25 August of 1944, there was an uprising of Parisians. This order came from Col Rol Tanguy and De Gaulle's emissaries. It took place in Paris. This bravery opened the way for the allies to enter. American, British, Senegalese and Canadian troops received welcome by Parisians. We placed all of our trust in these hallowed saviors of our freedom. They fought gallantly for days. The *French Second Armored Division* tanks, under General Leclerc's command, came strongly into Paris. These were the first Allied Forces to enter as the Germans surrendered at last!

By mid-August in 1944, the Allied control over Northwestern France allowed their penetration quickly into additional French territory. Finally, others bravely risked their lives to help us. At the same time, Soviets invaded Germany's Eastern border. Hitler was forced to order his troops to leave Southern France and Paris.

Has the tide actually changed at last? Will it hold? We prayed it was true. That same year of 1944 on 25 of August, finally, all German troops evacuated Paris. German General Dietrich von Choltitz signaled for surrender at the *Montparnasse Station* where General Leclerc and Col. Rol Tanguy gathered. On that same day, in *Hotel de Ville*, General Charles de Gaulle addressed his people. With a clear voice, General de Gaulle's words rang proudly to the French as he wished his people success and a genuine thank you! He ended by referring to Paris as the eternal city.

A little later in the day, the French and Allied troops marched together down the *Champ Elysees* to the roar of support. Now, all of Paris ran into the streets unafraid. Neighbors who had not seen each other in months fell into each other's arms merely happy to be alive. There was such great joy!

The shouts from the streets outside the La Fontaine mansion penetrated the thick fortress surrounding me. I stood alone by the General's old radio in the little guest house and cried. The tears choked my eyes, nose and throat. Stopping them was impossible. Once I allowed them to begin, it was as though something inside of me broke. Finally, I fell to my knees and raised my eyes to God. VieVie would not leave my mind!

What is she saying to me? "What has she done? Dear God, I know now our girl is broken. She was never right. We all knew it. The dear

General tried to tell me, but I did not watch over her. She should never have been allowed to leave her home. VieVie is frail and broken. What have we done to her? How can I help her? Amélie has strong arms to enfold and protect her. VieVie has nothing, nor do I."

Sobbing and thrashing on the floor, I didn't care. It shouldn't matter if I appeared weak. Tears mixed with snot as I screamed with pain for my dear girl. What good was it even continuing? Life was nothing to me. Suddenly, there was a knock on my house. I ignored it, but the intrusion would not stop. Over and over, someone gently tapped the massive door. Wiping my face with my dirty sleeve, I stumbled from the floor and fell toward the entrance. A little boy stood before me. He was as soiled as I, and the grime on his face was streaked, as was mine, with tears, but his expression was elated!

"Monsieur La Fontaine, you have not yet heard the news? It is over! The war is finally over. The allied and our French troops are cheering in the streets. Our mighty Resistance Fighters are coming home. Many brave allies are here, sir! Yes, many are here already! It is over. You must join us. Please, Monsieur take my hand. Run to see the *joie* upon all of the faces. If only the great General La Fontaine could see us; where is his beautiful wife? We all want you to come with us, your neighbors. How can you sit here alone? What is happening in our town is history, Monsieur! You will be most sad if you don't experience it with us. Now, come!"

The little guy grabbed my hand pulling me from the shadows of my prison. 19 August 1944, it was a spectacular day. The blue sky could only draw at the sadness of my spirit. Still, the farther I walked with the little boy, the more the tentacles of suffering became stripped from my soul. Happiness flowed in the streets. Soldiers kissed unknown French beauties as everyone felt joy unlike any they had ever experienced. Life, as we once knew and love, waited for us. Hell was almost finished. Any thoughts of remorse flew from my mind. That little boy pulled me from the clutches of possible death to the realization I was starving. Picking the wee lad up, I jumped with him into the air as far as my weakened state would allow which wasn't far. There was no room left in Paris for sadness. Let Amélie waddle in the arms of Gab, I no longer cared. Indeed, I *would* live. How foolish to experience the brink of disaster and not delight in the triumphant recovery.

Soon, Pierre's parents ran to us. I well remembered them. Often, they had stared at VieVie and me with great disdain. We thought they hated us but maybe not. In fact, perhaps Mrs. La Fontaine *would* be forgiven as well. How could anyone hate another for desiring to live? Undoubtedly, VieVie would receive penance and life would continue for her here in this mansion which she loved. Eventually, the truth would rise to the surface. Without a doubt, yes, VieVie La Fontaine would be forgiven!

I prayed, with all of my heart, this would occur. Deep inside, I realized the folly of my wishes. The locals would not overlook VieVie's indiscretions. They could not understand how noble her actions were. VieVie would never tell them her true role. Never would she chance harming others. *She is doomed!*

CHAPTER TWENTY-SIX

NOT SO FOR THE COLLABORATORS

Almost a day later, I made a promise to myself; I would never allow the pain which I earlier experienced to wrack my life. At one point, I had considered killing myself, but a little boy's hand pulled me back to the brink of living. Paris, on this late summer evening, appeared glorious. Again, I strolled the streets, filled with Parisians, as I held the small hand of the lad. Even though my depression lifted, I found myself desiring to return to my bed for a few more hours, but the little boy kept pulling me forward. Finally, I freed myself from the child and wandered home. *Where is VieVie?*

All of the Germans had fled from our city. She should be home. I checked her front door late last night, but it was still locked. Ambling cautiously in the dimming sun, I rattled the doorknob only to discover there was no change. I scratched my head over the perplexing question. I wondered. *Where is VieVie?*

As I began my trek toward my little house and probably a few more hours of sleep, someone startled me by grabbing my shoulder. Turning with confusion, I faced Madame Moreau, the mother of my new friend, the little Pierre. Her appearance shocked me. Only a while ago, her look was well-groomed but not now. Her silver hair stood up all over her head. Small, slits of eyes looked at me from swollen eyelids. Something terrible had occurred. *Is it Pierre?*

"Madame Moreau is everything okay? Has something happened to Pierre?" She felt too overcome with emotion to answer. Instead, she sadly took my right hand and led me out of the massive wrought-iron gate. Without a word, we hurried down the street. She began to run. I could only follow. Citizens continued to party and congregate in the streets. Just a while ago, I kissed many young women so that my lips hurt. Naturally, Madame Moreau did not know I planned to allow no more pain into my life. *Has my commitment to happiness ended so quickly?*

As we walked, the older lady's appearance was so shocking many turned to face her, but she had no concern over such trivial things. As we continued running down the *No. 3 rue Royale in the 8th arrondissement* toward Maxim's, briefly, my mind turned to Amélie, but I quickly removed her from my thoughts.

Poor Pierre, something dreadful must have happened. Why would the Madame Moreau desire me to accompany her? Pierre had a father and a few older brothers. My weakened state would not allow me to run much farther. The night was upon us. When I could see Maxim's, Madame turned down a little alley. It smelled of old, stale liquor and was very dirty. Ahead, I noticed a group of people, mostly men. Loud yells assaulted the air. What a frenzied group this was of whom I wanted no part. Quickly, I pulled my arm from my neighbor and shook my head.

"Please tell me what this is about, or I'm going home. I am so weak I can barely stand. I am going home!" Loud wails assaulted the air as my companion began to scream.

"I caused this. Oh, Monsieur, please assist. What they did here is *my* fault. I didn't realize this would happen. All over Paris, these French women, who were whores to the Germans, received a little retaliation. Sometimes, they shaved their heads, or they drew a swastika with bright lipstick but not this. I would never want Mrs. La Fontaine to suffer such as this. It is all *my* fault, but I don't know what to do. They won't stop. I think they raped her many times before I found her. Look what they have done. I once hated this woman when her saintly husband, General La Fontaine, died for this country but not to this degree. Make them stop Monsieur! Please!" The angry mob of men and a few Parisian women turned to me.

"Do *you* know this whore? Maybe, we got carried away, but you know she deserved it. Her husband was noble; she is only another slut!" Pushing the crowd aside, I faltered as I looked at a small figure lying in the nasty street. This group of angry men had roughly shaved the tiny form's beautiful spun golden hair. A few shreds of it remained which was grotesque as the thin layers stood straight up into the air. They beat, beyond recognition, the eyes of azure which I adored. Purple, blue, black sheets of severe bruising looked as though there were no eyes there. The sad object's face was dirty and smeared with red lipstick from a bright red swastika painted onto the small forehead. The blue dress, which she wore, was once beautiful but now hung in shards of rags on her exquisite, small frame. Softly, the soiled, broken doll moaned.

No longer could I cry. I had shed many tears during our occupation; there were none left. "You have no idea what you have done." My angry yells assaulted the little alley.

"Yes, we do! She is a whore for the Germans. We refuse to allow her to live among us. Many people say she has always preferred Germans. Year ago, during her youth, she took a German lover right under the dear General's nose. Well, let her go back to Germany and her beloved Nazi men. They can have her! This whore is a collaborator. We will search them out and take care of them, all of them!" As I kneeled beside her, the tears *did* start uncontrollably. Her small body lay in an unnatural position. She suffered several broken bones as well as deep lacerations. Cradling her head gently into my arms, I shielded her from the crowd.

"Oh, VieVie, my love, what have they done to you?" A few tears escaped the swollen space, but her eyes were too damaged to cry. A guttural sound escaped her throat. My precious love attempted to speak but was unable. Most likely, these brutes crushed her larynx. Briefly, she reached to me. For the longest time, I held her and cried. The crowd quietened in confusion. Madame Moreau continued to shriek. Knowing I shouldn't move her, I couldn't help myself. As a parent rocks a small child, I rocked her as gently as possible. The sounds from her stopped. Finally, I pulled away. Getting help at once was imperative.

I must get her to a hôpital immediately! As I pulled away from her, she fell slowly onto the street. VieVie La Fontaine was dead.

For a very long time, I tried to convince myself the heap lying on the dirty sidewalk was *not* my love. Her face appeared deformed from the blows, and her golden hair was gone. No, this could not be the beautiful VieVie La Fontaine. This little creature was a monster, horrid. As quickly as denial overcame me, I plunged into anger.

Shocked she could be gone, I sobbed as a wounded animal. I continued to stand in the same spot for the longest time. My eyes refused to leave the small form heaped on the soiled street. Through my tears, I looked at the only woman whom I ever valued. At that moment, I realized I could never love again. As though in a trance, my mind ran a quick retake of all of the vital moments which I shared with my VieVie.

Alone you lie, no more will I love you. Alone you lie, no more will I smell the glorious vanilla scent which always surrounds you. Alone you lie, no more will I spy the golden spun honey of your hair. Alone you lie, no more will I look at the alabaster skin which shields you. Alone you lie, no more will I see the eyes of bluest blue. Alone you lie, no more will I enjoy the laughter of joy from living in your beloved Paris. Alone you lie, crushed and dirty but to me, you are an angel of unbeknown love. Alone you lie, but I will always love only you. Boiling anger raged through my veins as my heart broke into a million pieces.

My rage is her fault! She caused me to react! If she had not insisted we do something noble, then this would not have occurred. We should have played it safe like these animals I face who hid in their safe houses. No, not VieVie La Fontaine, she had to be noble. Never had I known such anger. I heard my shrieks as though from a wild animal. Briefly, I became an animal who was savage and broken as I hurled the words into the air.

"Alone you lie!" Then I turned in desperation to the small crowd who looked at me with confusion.

"You don't know what you have done! You angry beasts, how could you assault this woman. How long have you held her in captivity and had your way with her?"

"Don't you know who she is?" Shuddering as a madman, I charged the group. They ran back a little. One of the men stopped. He held a club. The look on his face appeared crazed.

"What are you a lover of German whores? This woman was an imposter. She's no French lady. She is a German of the worst kind. The word is not only did she court a German as a lover years ago but lately, she has entertained a German Jew. This woman, your friend, Mrs. Moreau, told us all about *this* miserable piece. She deserved everything we did to her. How do you know she didn't enjoy some of it?" With those words of an indictment, Mrs. Moreau increased her screams.

The group standing in front of me reminded me of the savagery and ruthlessness of the Germans. I shook my head. "How can you feel sorry for her when so many soldiers died trying to defend all of us? What about our brave Resistance Fighters, what do you think *they* would feel if they faced her? They would do worse than this." He pointed at the small woman who lied in the street like a piece of trash.

"You see, I feel sorry for *you*. For all of you because my answer, you will never be able to forget. This woman was once beautiful. She loved life, but most of all, she *loved France*. You see, this woman *was* the Resistance. VieVie La Fontaine was a French Resistance Fighter. Her role was the most dangerous. Why didn't you take her to trial? The truth would have shocked you. When most of you fearfully huddled safely in your houses, she slept with the brutes. The very people she detested, she agreed to allow them to paw at her body so she could glean vital information. They broke her free and shining spirit. Those despicable animals took the rest of her humanity. She was never perfect, but she loved life and France. She gave her *life* for France, for you. You have killed the Star of the Resistance. I hope you are content now. I beg you to stop this vigilante spree. Wait for the Resistance to confirm their soldiers. You have made a most vile mistake here. How many others have you ignorantly punished?"

Sobs and apologies meekly were offered as I picked my love from the alley. Gently, I carried her down the street as word spread before us of what had occurred. Many of the men removed their hats and held them to their hearts. Women tossed flowers into my path. All of this, I could see from within the tears.

My heart will never be the same.

CHAPTER TWENTY-SEVEN

A NEW LIFE ALONE

Alone, I stayed at the La Fontaine guest house. No longer did I live. Now, I only *remained*. There was no gentle laughter, nor any hope of it ever again. All I did once more was sleep. Madame Moreau placed small parcels of food on my front step as she had once before when I waited alone for the return of my angel. At least, for a time, there remained hope. No longer was I granted that beacon so necessary to continue.

Outside, in the streets of "Gay Paree," life was indeed happy again. Clean up began as people worked to clear the roads. Fears evaporated for most. Not for Mark Lichter although I was able to assume my real name without fear of reprisal. Was there any real future security for one such as I? No longer would I have dreams of the beautiful VieVie. I now dreamed of a *land* which would comfort and delight me. Did a place exist where I could receive welcome with the assurance I didn't need to change my very identity to live? *Was* there a land where innocent souls were not herded as cattle into boxcars because they were Jewish?

Once the authorities claimed the body of VieVie, I heard nothing more of her. These officials issued no arrest warrants for those who tortured her. It was as though she did not exist. Madame Moreau bowed her head whenever I opened the door at her stirring as she nursed me earlier in the absence of the La Fontaine's, she did so once again.

My complete devastation was the result of more than the loss of the two women whom I loved. Knowing Amélie rested in the arms of Gabriel, the man whom she *truly* loved, gave me a little peace and joy. VieVie's loss, however, consumed me. The tears which I shed seemed never to end. For the longest time, just the thought of her face caused me to break down with indescribable grief. Eventually, I realized the pain which wracked me was more profound than *her* loss. I mourned for the fact humanity could be void of moral goodness. After all the destruction the French suffered, how could a group of respectable citizens take it into their hands to reap such agony on one as beautiful as VieVie? Would you not assume they may finally discover human compassion? How could they not have waited for the return of the Resistance? Easily, those men could have brought VieVie to trial as a collaborator. Then, the Resistance would have defended her as they offered a reason for her actions.

Madame La Fontaine was not a collaborator. No, she was the Resistance! Those words would have cleared all charges, and my beauty would walk with me still.

Often, I tried to imagine what it must have entailed living with the enemy. Sharing not only most of her meals, joy, pain, and fears with a group of men whom she hated. The nationality who killed her husband and attacked her homeland. What was it like to sleep with someone who was the very soul of all you resented? The pain which enveloped her would eventually strip her of all emotions. I prayed she might have been so devoid of emotions that perhaps, she felt no pain at her assault although I reasoned this was not so.

Oh, my dearest, sweet girl how did you survive? Was it thoughts of your beloved Paris? Did the face of the adored General push you into the performance of your life? Could I have possibly played into the strength which you developed to act your role each day? I can only imagine the nights must have consumed you.

I couldn't help but also think of my parents. Should I return to Germany and claim my rightful home, my Father's law office and all of their other assets? Deep depression prevented me from acting in any way other than eating and sleeping. So I waited.

Early one morning, there was a knock on the door. Two officials stared into my small house. Yawning with aggravation, I opened the door a little to peer at them. Kindly, they introduced themselves. Explaining they were representatives of General La Fontaine, I invited them inside. Respectfully, they requested my documentation which I had earlier removed from the main house and hidden in my bedroom. After I provided all they asked, they departed hastily. My fears again flared. Had I done the wrong thing? Now, I waited for steps to cart me away for living in the home of a General as well as providing a false identity earlier. *Well, ole boy, you should just give it up. You are royally screwed.*

Lately, I spent most of my time in the bedroom by the window. I had repositioned my easel from the studio to the bedroom. My energy felt drained but at least with the easel there; I dabbed a little paint now and again onto the large canvas. Early each morning and late in the afternoon, when cocktails and laughter had once surrounded our easels, I painted alone. Not for very long, but briefly I did what once stirred such joy in my chest.

Slowly, I witnessed the rebirth of a gift. The painting of large green platanes made me smile. The light on my canvas appeared spectacular. Never in the past was I able to capture the weaving in and out of the sun as the healthy green plants now came to life on my canvas. A spark of hope ignited inside my weary spirit. Possibly, there could be life without VieVie, but it would be a sad and weary one. My broken mind no longer functioned normally. Now, I could never make vague promises of not suffering pain as I had done so foolishly in the past. Instead, I must be able to live with the agonizing guilt; I failed the only woman whom I ever loved or could love as well as my parents *and* the General.

Standing in front of my easel in the waning evening light, a knock on the door carried me back to reality. Staggering toward the wooden structure, I opened it without regard to my intruder. An official-looking gentleman nodded his head for entry. I opened my door widely. Mr. Miller explained he also represented General La Fontaine who was his client. The General had left a will. Upon the unlikely demise of his wife, the only heir, I should inherit the La Fontaine fortune.

Such news caused me to stagger into the wall. Light-headedness reminded me I hadn't eaten well in some time. Mr. Miller extended a handful of keys as he offered his remorse at my loss. Not knowing what to do, I took the keys. My visitor left. Again, I remained alone. Once more, I had received a blessing from others as well as the fact my now home remained unscathed from the bombs and vandals of Paris.

Several days passed until I was able to process the news. Before I entered the main house, I contacted the officials in Germany about receiving all my parents also left behind. They requested documentation which I sent with a representative to Berlin. Now, I walked to the La Fontaine house where so many emotions silently waited for recognition.

I entered the massive door as in the past. Thoughts flooded my mind of the General as he enjoyed reading his newspaper in the sunny location at the table on my first entry long ago. I walked to *that* spot and reached out to the memory which sat in his chair. Laughing, I recalled Anne-Laure and the massive breakfast she provided on our first morning years earlier. Stooping, I kneeled to the floor where I fell in tears at the news: I could never return to Berlin. Those were my parent's wishes.

Okay, one thing was clear. I would *not* go back to Germany. Instead, I would sell the house and office there. Then, I would request a check for all of the assets which my parents worked diligently to save for me. Now, sadly, I glanced around me at all these possessions which another family so generously left me.

Careful not to fall, I began to stand in the spot where VieVie gently assisted me into my chair. Her face, the face of an angel, had enveloped me in the scent of sweet vanilla. As that thought flooded my senses, I reached toward the vision before me. There was nothing. What was I to do with all of this? Suddenly, it became clear. The first thing was to establish a memorial to the General and his brave wife, VieVie La Fontaine.

All of France and Europe would hear of the bravery not only from the General but also of his Resistance Fighter wife. Finally, I was able to smile. Not only was I now a wealthy man, but I also had a noble purpose. Such dedicated work would be necessary to shed light on these two heroes of the Second World War. After I completed that mission, I would establish a memorial to the Jews of France and all of the Holocaust survivors as well as the French Resistance Fighters.

For many months, I diligently worked as I uncovered tidbits of the lives of the General and his young wife. It broke my heart to learn of the history of my little love. Louie La Fontaine was born into extreme wealth. Not so for his wife, who always struggled with her identity. Her lot was not easy. It appeared she never knew her parents but was herded from home to home early in her childhood. I discovered a little photo book from the General in which he assembled photos of them as they dated. He made notes. His parents had not approved of his choice of a bride. They detested her. Sadly, the General had written down the scathing comments of his parents and their inhospitable treatment of the woman whom he adored. VieVie was forced to live in the guest house for one year before the General was able to marry her with some degree of his parent's blessing. Eventually, she won their hearts as she did for anyone whom she desired to love. Wedding day photos displayed happy, smiling faces as his parents scowled in the background.

VieVie, you were tiny. You look like a little girl. What a sad and complicated life she had lived. A young girl who never experienced the love of her father now faced the remainder of time scarred by his actions. Her strange actions began to make sense to me. How could she not struggle with her identity? All she wanted was the love of her father. Hence, the marriage to an older man who sheltered her and provided her with the closest thing to unconditional love. All of these facts also explained her fascination with men, any man. My father, me, as well as all the others, it all fell into place as I began to understand the pieces of her broken life. *Alone you lie but never forgotten, my dearest love.*

CHAPTER TWENTY-EIGHT
EXILED

The year was 1945 when Joseph Darnand, the brute who had donned a Waffen SS uniform while he headed the militia which waged war on our French Resistance alongside the Germans, was put on trial for his life. He stated, he did not fear the *real* resistance but those who pretended to belong to the illustrious group.

People of France and Europe began to hail the Resistance Fighters as heroes. Wherever I walked, people desired to touch me or to talk about the war. Many citizens, who never enlisted in our great cause, now pretended they *had* fought as Resistance Fighters. Their actions did not disturb me. Such was expected. I realized the feelings of shame and of fear which resulted from hiding in safety while those around you perished. Yes, I knew those feelings well.

Diligently, I worked to establish a monument of worth for two people who deserved remembrance. The local cemetery welcomed my plans as we worked to develop more than a marble figurehead but a peaceful solace under the large, green platane trees which Paris loved.

The monument to the General and VieVie made me proud. I hoped they approved from their lofty station in Heaven. Often, I visited *that* place and talked to my beloved two fallen friends. My Holocaust Memorial also pleased me as I watched hundreds of people pay respect to the innocents. Their respect soothed my soul. Time passed uneventfully for me as peace finally began to shield me. More silver threaded among the darkness of my hair. Appearances no longer mattered, not to me.

In France, at the end of WWII, the devastation was widespread as families lost beloved members and their entire life savings. The German occupation destroyed our beloved country. The most crucial question facing France in 1945 was "how to rebuild?" Not only her homes but the entire government must be redesigned and reestablished.

In that regard, I knew how blessed I was to have a home where I was safe. At last, the news came from Berlin, my parent's house received severe damages. There was no chance of repair, and the Nazis had destroyed Father's office. This news did not bother me. I owned the land. It must be worth something? My Father's attorney was tracking down their assets. Many Germans had transferred assets to Switzerland. I hoped Hans and Abi had done so, but it didn't matter. None of this concerned me either. The kindness of the La Fontaine's would provide a sweet life for me. Never would I be able to spend it all.

Living felt good again but lonely. Conditions were once more becoming peaceful in France. The losses of most of the country were staggering. We all did what we could to assist each other. Years ticked forward while I waited to hear from my family's attorney in Berlin. Due to the volume of requests from so many, I expected this would take a very long time to settle. That was fine. Plenty of days waited patiently for me.

The year was 1947, I sat early in the morning, reading my newspaper in the chair the General assigned to me so long ago. Delicious French roast coffee awakened my senses as my housekeeper silently worked in the kitchen. Harriet assisted me by thoughtfully running my household. Brightly, she entered with a smile from her jaunt to the mailbox. As she lay the mail by my right hand, she picked up my bone china, white cup for a refill. Without regard, I picked up her deposit of daily mail and glanced through it. Waiting for attention was a post from Germany. Once I opened the letter, I smiled. News from Germany, for once, appeared pleasant. The German officials finally settled my earlier requests for closing my parent's estate. The land possessed more value than I hoped and of course, diligent Hans and Abi had indeed transferred most of their money to a bank in neutral Switzerland. I received a wire transfer in an amount which surprised me more quickly than I could have imagined from the country which had not entered the war.

Never had I been aware of the vast wealth of my family. All of this news was good. A trip to Berlin was not necessary for me. The thought of visiting the location of my family home did not appeal to me. I desired to remember happier times. What good would it do for me to wallow in the guilt and loss which waited there?

With a faraway look, I picked up the statement from my bank and studied the amount. It occurred to me: I now owned two homes, but none gave me peace. Staying here, in the estate of VieVie and the General, would keep me living in the past as if I returned to Germany. If I was to find any joy, I needed to discover *my* way. Did not a place in the entire world exist which might welcome one such as I?

My wealth was staggering. There was much good I could accomplish but where? A land must exist that would welcome me and reach out to provide a feeling of belonging with kindred souls. Was there a place where Jews belonged? A voice in my head softly whispered, *"Exile."*

Exile? Yes, I had heard that word before. I repeated the word. Already in my life, I had faced the uncertainty of a new life in a strange land by myself. Things had turned out better for me than most of the residents in France and Germany. If only there were a place where I could age without fear of being uprooted and running for my life again. Then, the unforgettable happened.

In July 1947, the *President Warfield Ship* left *Sète*, France, for Palestine. It carried over four thousand five-hundred Jewish men, women and children, all displaced persons (DPs) or survivors of the Holocaust. Before the ship (by then renamed the *Exodus* 1947) could reach Palestine's territorial waters, British destroyers surrounded it. On 18 July, British naval forces struggled with passengers on the ship. The British troops killed a crew member and two passengers. Many other passengers suffered bullet wounds and other injuries.

The British towed the ship to *Haifa* and transferred the passengers onto three navy means of transports which returned to Europe. Their goal was to make an example of the *Exodus* 1947. They finally landed in *Port-de-Bouc*, France. There the passengers were ordered to disembark, but the French authorities refused to remove these refugees forcibly. British authorities feared adverse public opinion. They decided to wait until the passengers disembarked of their own accord. The "waiting game" did not fare well for the British. These passengers, including many orphaned children, forced the issue by declaring a hunger strike. Despite terrible suffering already inflicted upon them, they gallantly waited without food, some for over twenty-one days. Thankfully, they did consume water. Their bravery and commitment received considerable attention to the dire situation. Pressure mounted from the international media coverage which pressed British authorities to find a solution before passengers died. Just the same, the ship sat for three additional weeks in the sweltering summer heat. Still, the brave passengers refused to disembark voluntarily, and the French authorities were unwilling to force them to leave. At last, the British government transported the passengers to *Hamburg*. Much to everyone's shock, the passengers were then interned in camps within the British zone of occupation in Germany.

How can this occur? All over Europe, displaced persons protested vociferously and staged hunger strikes once they heard the news. Great protests erupted on both sides of the Atlantic. All of this humiliated Britain. Such an event played a significant role in the diplomatic swing of sympathy toward the Jews. At last, there was recognition of a Jewish State in 1948. The Jews finally had a place which they could call "home."

Reading of this news created a stirring in our very souls, the souls of the Jewish people. It was as if God spoke to us. My problem settled through no actions of my own. *Israel must be the answer.* Hungrily, I read of this new country.

On 15 May 1948, the ongoing civil war transformed into an interstate conflict between Israel and the Arab states. After this, the Israeli Government boldly declared independence. A combined invasion by Egypt, Jordan and Syria, together with expeditionary forces from Iraq, entered Palestine. Jordan had stated privately to *Yishuv* emissaries on 2 May; it would abide by a decision not to attack the Jewish State. These other invading forces took control of the Arab areas. Together, they immediately attacked Israeli soldiers and several Jewish settlements. These actions resulted in ten months of fighting. Twice these fights were interrupted by several truce periods. Mainly, these took place within the former territory of the British Mandate as well as in the Sinai Peninsula and Southern Lebanon.

War no longer frightened me! To the contrary, I desired to battle once again. My fate, no my very life, would become Israel. There, I would spend my remaining days helping to establish a land which would welcome all people but especially *my* people, the Jews. With plenty of money, I surely would be able to build a life for myself as well as help many others.

In 1949, Israel signed separate armistices: with Egypt on 24 February; Lebanon on 23 March; Jordan on 3 April; and Syria on 20 July. Fervently, I read my Hebrew Bible as I desired to understand the complicated history of my new homeland, *Israel*. The sound of it rolled off my tongue. Immediately, I put all of the La Fontaine property on the market as I began to pack. Quickly, a lovely American family purchased my home. This family came to help in the rebuilding of France from New York. The wife of this entrepreneur was French.

"I am free!" My words resounded in the darkness of the night on the signing of the contract for the sale of the La Fontaine's beautiful home. Memories of VieVie and the General, I told myself, would remain *here*. This place where we shared so much pain but also a great deal of joy. Standing in the library, I remembered the night when VieVie and I entered drenched from the profuse rain. Thoughts of making love to her for the first time were allowed again into my memory. My VieVie existed on a podium so high, I had not granted my mind access to any thought which did not honor her. With my new freedom, I realized *these* ordinary memories entailed the essence of the woman. She would have desired me to remember not only her final days of undeserved torment but of happier times when she was carefree, when she was indeed, *VieVie La Fontaine!*

All of my plans finally were completed for my exit to Israel. My heart soared as I tried to imagine what waited for me. For many weeks, I had read my Hebrew Bible which I studied each night. Of course, I also considered current books on the land and even real estate available for sale in Jerusalem. My dream at this point was to live there amongst the ancient history of my people. Saying those words made me shiver.

Will this land welcome me? I must change residency as soon as I arrive at my new home. Gladly, I will bear arms for my chosen country. If I was willing to fight to the death for Paris, how much more for a land which desires me?

Dreamily, I existed while I dreamed of the place waiting to embrace me, which waited to breathe life into a tired, dejected soul. As in the days of the Bible, I dreamed of walking sacred paths and touching ancient architecture. Profoundly, my lungs would expand as I imagined the unpolluted air of old Jerusalem. This place of varied languages and cultures. All of these thoughts created unknown excitement in my heart.

Two days before my scheduled departure, as an afterthought, I went next door. It had been weeks since I had seen Madame Moreau and her family working outside in her lovely gardens. This situation was extremely odd. They were usually outdoors for most of the day as little Pierre ran and played on his outdoor toys. The little guy and I lately had become quite close. I frequently took him to lunch or a local park. However, I noticed something was going on between his mother and father which I didn't understand. I could feel the ice between them whenever I visited. This tension made me want to rush from their presence. The way Mr. Moreau glared at me created profound discomfort for me, but my little buddy, Pierre, didn't seem aware of any problems. Pierre always ran to my arms with such joy!

Happily, I strutted to their door with the excitement of my news. The Moreau's must be aware the La Fontaine home was listed on the market. Evidently, they had heard by now the property sold quickly. It was strange to me the Madame had not stopped to inquire as to my plans.

When I stepped onto the porch, I knew. *Something is most wrong here. I hope it isn't little Pierre suffering from a problem.* As I rang the doorbell, I pressed my head to the glass. A great deal of sunlight flooded the entrance hall. This space was large and nicely decorated except things were a mess! Never, had I seen Madame Moreau's home short of perfection. *Yes, something is most wrong!*

The radio blared French music. Dead flower arrangements scattered around the area. Had someone died? The look was depressing. Finally, I began to beat on the door. Now, I was frightened for the little boy.

As I beat on the door, the form of a man approached. Angrily, he thrust open the door. He grimaced at me. Apparently, the brightness of the day hurt his eyes. He was disheveled and looked as though he had not seen daylight in a long time. "Monsieur Moreau is everything okay? I stopped by to explain I am moving soon. Pierre and I have become rather close. It seems important Pierre hear this news directly from me."

From behind the door, I heard the whimpering of a small child. *Is Pierre injured? Has his father hit him?* With no regard to the large man blocking my entrance, I pushed the door right into the father's head. Mr. Moreau staggered backward. He was already drunk at this early morning hour. The same angry glare as before assaulted me.

Quickly, I entered to find the little boy sitting alone behind the door. His little face streaked with tears and mucus from his nose. While he reached his small arms into the air, I looked at him with fatherly love.

I have not considered how important this wee lad has become to my life. Gently, I bent toward him and scooped him into my arms. His little hands clasped my neck as his small body shivered with emotion.

"Oh, please, Monsieur, do not leave me alone here. My Mama is very ill, and Papa no longer is happy. You are all I have in this world. My brothers left weeks ago to live with my aunt, but Mama wouldn't let me. May I live with you? Please, sir." His request was a whisper as he kept his eyes down.

"For heaven's sakes, Monsieur Moreau what is going on here? Where is the boy's mama? May I see her?"

"So, you are leaving? The 'mighty hero of the Resistance' is bolting on us? My wife talked about you for so long. I got sick of it. Everyone in Paris hates my wife for what she did to *your* Madame La Fontaine. People shun the boy and me as well. Do me a tremendous favor and take them with you to wherever you go. Maybe, then, I can have a life. My other boys suffer because of the ignorance of a woman with a gossipy tongue."

Mr. Moreau plodded toward the sofa which was surrounded by newspapers and empty bottles of gin. I held little Pierre firmly to my chest. He was dirty and seemed to have a head cold. My heart broke for the one person who had reached out to me at the worst time in *my* life. If he had not beckoned for me to join him as he celebrated so long ago at the liberation of Paris, I might have ended my life. At this very moment, I desired to help the boy as he once did for me.

"Oh, please, sir may I accompany you? Please, don't leave me here. Mama cries all of the time, and Papa is angry at me. He hates me. I am hungry. No one wants to help me. Please let me go with you. I promise I will be good." His words followed by soft whimpering.

Again, the small arms enfolded around my neck with a tight embrace. I was unsure what to do but knew I must help my little friend. Since I decided a long time ago I would never marry, he may be the son which I denied myself. As I stood, trying to determine my next move, Mrs. Moreau walked into my presence. Her appearance was more shocking than the day when she led me to poor VieVie in the streets surrounded by her killers. Shockingly, I looked into her swollen eyes.

"Please, Mr. Lichter, will you take Pierre? His life here in Paris is doomed. No one will let their children play with him. Our family may as well be dead. In fact, death is an option which grows more pleasant for me. Will you help me? Of course, I realize my asking help from you is quite a great deal since I am responsible for the death of your aunt."

She hung her head. I was pretty sure she knew the depth of my involvement with Mrs. La Fontaine but appreciated the generosity in her statement. My next words shocked me. Never had I even considered such a preposterous thing!

"Why don't you join me in my flight from Paris? You and Pierre will live with me in a place called, Israel. The people there will accept all of us. Yes, please come with me. You and Pierre will be the family that I never expected. I mean this as I ask you both earnestly to join me."

Pierre clapped his little hands. Then, he placed a small one on each of my cheeks and kissed me. Suddenly, he transformed into the little boy of yesteryear. The one who always appeared happy. Even the bleakness of Mrs. Moreau changed at my words. We all turned to look at the slovenly husband. He sat up, inspired by my words to leave his drunken stupor.

"You want them? Take them but know you are now responsible for both of them. She's a decent cook, so at least you will get your money out of her, but don't expect much in the bed. Lotte is an old woman and sags everywhere. I doubt if you'll receive much inspiration in that department." Poor Mrs. Moreau bowed her head in shame.

Falling back onto the sofa, he looked at me in disbelief that I may consider such a ridiculous move as taking his wife and child into my care. Well, not only did I think about it. We did!

"You must pack now. I arranged my day of departure within two days, but I may need to extend the time to accommodate *my* new family. Oh, Mrs. Moreau and Pierre, I am ecstatic you will join me. I have studied this new land named Israel. It will welcome such as us. Now, cheer up! I'll call later this evening with the exact time for departure."

I kissed them each on the cheek. Madame Moreau would be the mother I no longer had and Pierre would fill the hole in my heart for a son. This happiness was the best news which I had received in such a long time.

CHAPTER TWENTY-NINE

ISRAEL

Our flight from Tel Aviv to Jerusalem lasted a little over thirty-four minutes. We all lightly traveled as I had done on my trip from Berlin to Paris more than fifteen years earlier. Landing in Tel Aviv, all I desired was to visit Jerusalem and possibly find a home. Since there were no flights into the sacred city, I decided to relax and figure everything out as I went. Where *would* I finally settle? Joyfully, I smiled as I remembered a young boy who once traveled alone from what he believed was safety and security in Berlin after a horrible war to the spectacle of Paris. Father had warned me at that time to travel lightly.

You don't want to stand out, Mark. Once you arrive, purchase new clothes so you will fit into your adopted culture. Again, I heeded his words as I arrived with just the same small, brown satchel. Pierre and his mama each carried only one bag as well. Pierre slept on the plane. He must have been exhausted from all of the stress. Mrs. Moreau looked around her with great happiness as she observed everything. In my mind, I pictured us living in a small house in the old section of the holy city. Prolific reading of late reinforced my dream.

Oh, dear Jerusalem, I can't wait to walk among your ancient streets and breathe the subtropical, semiarid air in your warm, dry summers and chilly, rainy winters! To live amongst people who welcome and identify with me. Can this be?

The vision of my small cottage right in the middle of Jerusalem made me smile. Each day, I would walk her streets and touch ancient stones. My reading disclosed how dangerous driving in this city of mixed cultures could become. The roads were described as "narrow and torturous" in my books. Well, at least driving was on the right side of the road if ever I did feel brave enough to drive.

Dreams of blessed Israel were pushed away by the sound of the pilot as we rapidly descended into the Ben Gurion airport in Tel Aviv which was fifty kilometers north of *my* Jerusalem.

My little family grabbed our luggage and almost ran from the plane as quickly as the lines would allow. We all had our documentation ready for the authorities. My plans for making this our home expedited the procedure of clearing customs. Soon enough, we walked into the glorious day. On this August day, we received welcome by the perfect temperature of seventy-five degrees which was the mean temperature for this time of year. I had read about the *sharav* and couldn't wait to experience it. This hot, dry, desert wind is typical in Israel both in the autumn and spring. The word is Arabic for fifty days about the length of time which it blows each year. On *this* perfect day, there was no *sharay*. Instead, the humidity was about sixty-two percent which was extremely pleasant. Israelis experience unusual exposure to the sun's rays because of a lack of clouds and low humidity. Also, the sun reaches a higher angle.

The first thing I noticed was no severe air pollution. Fully, I breathed the intoxicating air surrounding me just as I once had dreamed. I never wanted to leave this place! As we walked toward an awaiting car and driver, I noticed the soil was red and brown as I had read was typical for the Mediterranean area.

Tears flowed from my eyes as they did from many others whom I passed on arrival as we looked at each other. *We are as one.* This place drew us from all over the world as none other ever had. Here, we weren't confined or scoffed; we received salutations of welcome. *Can this be?*

Conscription waited for me apparently as it did in Israel for all Israeli citizens over the age of eighteen. The average length of compulsory service in the military was around three years. Even though I felt much older than my thirty-three years, I could still serve. First, I must become a citizen of this land. Due to the *Law of Return*, my goal would be easily attainable because I was Jewish.

Immediately, my small family and I must select a house. So many exciting and promising actions waited for us. Smiles surrounded Lotte, Pierre and me as we climbed into the shiny, new Mercedes with our driver. My heart yearned to live in Jerusalem, but the practical side of me said, "Tel Aviv will be a better choice." *Which will win?*

When I saw Jerusalem, again I cried. Emotions unlike anything which I had experienced in a very long time waffled inside of me. I feared I would be disappointed, but the land was precisely as I had read and this place perfectly matched the pictures in my books. Pierre looked a little disappointed.

"Where is the water? My Papa said there would be water. He said you are rich. You will buy me a home on the beach. That is what I desire. Please, Mark, may we live at the beach?" Lotte looked at me sadly. *Way to go Mr. Moreau. Thank you for spoiling my dream.*

Although the driver tried to entice me into settling here, I didn't feel the pull I had dreamed would exist. Possibly, Pierre's words or perhaps I would have felt the disassociation with Jerusalem eventually.

We checked into our hotel. Then ordered room service. The room had adjoining doors so the little boy ran from my chamber to Lotte's with joy. Early the next day, we would search for the perfect residence in this new place. Tonight, we walked the streets and breathed the fresh air of this eternal city which sat on an elevation of two thousand seventy-five feet above sea level. From the East side of the town, we looked down on the Dead Sea. Pierre groaned.

"Mark, that's the only water? It is not pretty." He could not know the West side of the city faced the coastal plain and the Mediterranean Sea. At that point, I admitted I would gladly change my plans to make "my" little boy happy. I believed Lotte was so thrilled to be away from Paris and her drunken husband she didn't care. She never offered any opinion, so it would be up to Pierre and me to make such a nagging choice.

Early the next morning, we searched. The real estate agent was knowledgeable, but the place wasn't right for us. Later in the day, it dawned on me; we needed to return to Tel Aviv and look on the shores of the Mediterranean. Money was not an object. Giving joy to this family, *my family*, became my priority. So, later in the day, I thanked the agent and asked if she could direct us to someone in Tel Aviv.

"That would be my sister. We work together. She sells million dollar plus properties as interests you. Do you want to begin midmorning tomorrow?" Pierre screamed with glee. Lotte touched my hand with delight.

Is *this the life of Mark Lichter?* My good fortune made me feel humble. Early the next day, Hannah Ackermann met us at our hotel in Tel Aviv with the same smile as her sister the day before. Hannah was a high-pressure sales person, unlike the younger sister who had been very low-key. As we departed each house, I felt sorry I had not made an offer because they were all so lovely. The entire day, we searched. Pierre loved each possibility because they all sat on a gorgeous beach among some of the highest-dollar real estate in the world.

Eventually, what we chose is a little embarrassing, but I left the decision to Pierre who wanted the most substantial house. We made an offer that same evening on a ten thousand two-hundred twenty-six square foot house with fourteen rooms. I convinced myself we needed the space. Our six bedroom house had the same number of baths as well as an extra one. The exterior was grey Jerusalem stone. There existed three large attached garages. Already, Pierre claimed one in which to ride his future bike. Arab arches graced each door of this Templar style home. After I had signed the contract, Pierre and I walked outside by the statue which sprayed water high into the air. Happily, I remembered the home which VieVie had shared with me and the gorgeous fountain of the La Fontaine's. Now, I claimed *my* fountain and *my* family. Tears fell silently from tired eyes as I dipped my hand into the gentle mist. Pierre did the same. Were those tears on his little cheek or had the spray misted him?

We offered full price for the home of our dreams as Hannah frowned at us. I didn't care. Life was short. Negotiations would only have dragged out the process. We needed to get down to the delights which waited for us. Joys, better than any of my dreams, lingered for our displaced family of three who suffered so much.

Our new house came furnished, which sped up our moving. Once there, Pierre established many friends. Often, I watched as he proudly showed them "his" home. Well, it was *his* home. Lotte also settled quickly. The sound of women gaily laughing was a new sound. Never did I remember my mother entertaining other women or VieVie doing so for that matter. Life with my little family was dynamic and happy.

The three of us went to the beach each day as laughter echoed around us. Frequently, we took picnic lunches or played volleyball on the shore. Beautiful blue/green waters washed away any cares. Our favorite place was *Hilton Beach*.

There, water sports abounded. *The Sea Centre Club* offered windsurfing and kayaking classes. Pierre became an expert in each. Soon, he became my teacher on anything sports related. Many days, we left the picnic lunch at home and enjoyed one of the many delightful restaurants. This host of restaurants offered varied beach food which thrilled Pierre. Our time there drew us together. Quickly, we became a loving family. Three sad lives entwined into one happy, loving family. There were no secrets among us.

Proudly, I served my new country, Israel, after I finally received my summons to duty. The three years passed quickly. While I worked as a soldier, many life-long friends entered my happy world. I learned much about my new home. The time as a soldier delighted me. No longer did I feel as though I didn't belong. Here, I did. Slowly, the pain of subjection in Berlin and Paris decreased as I learned what it meant to enjoy life at the highest level.

My life has flown past since I arrived in this ancient land. Many joyous days have blessed me because of this land and the two people whom I love. Pierre is grown now and has given me two precious grandsons. Our large home filled with joy and activity. Sadly, Lotte passed away several years ago. Time is jumbled and runs together because today, I am an old man at ninety-five years old. So many memories flood my mind as I try to remember VieVie and Louie. It is difficult keeping all of the facts straight. Although Israeli life expectancy ranks among the world's highest, my life is finally waning. I don't mind, what a full and exciting life God has given me! The joy is he saved the best for last. Having a little boy to watch over and a mother figure to love me has been the best I could desire at least in this world.

In my old age, I have become obsessive. Each evening, I do the same thing. After my walk outside around my home, quietly I sit in my favorite chair as I stare at a giant blown-up photo which hangs prominently in my bedroom. I observe the figures of three young and happy people. The face and body of an angel smile at me as does her handsome husband, a famous French General. The other person is me. A young boy who has no idea what awaits him in life. This young lad expects it will not be well for him. How could he leave the love of his parents and his beloved homeland? With the help of God, the young German/Jewish man did the best that he could.

Finally, he forgave himself. At last, this man discovered a land where he belonged. Also in the photo is a blurred figure. For the longest time, I tried to distinguish the form. One evening, it became clear to me. The blurred image was a very pregnant Lotte. She had hurried over that evening long ago with fresh cookies to meet the nephew of her neighbors. I could barely remember the time. There stood my future mother and my future son still in her belly, but I did not know. I did not realize the love which would fill my chest each time I smiled into their faces. How strange are the actions of our God! Israel, the home I always dreamed to find is now my own, and I share it with those who love me and my God.

What more is there to life? Yes, what more is there to life!

The End